FRONTIERS OF LIBERTY

Three stories from America's struggle for independence

Shannon McNear

ShenandoahDawn

These novellas previously appeared in collections from Barbour Publishing, but have been updated and revised.

These are works of fiction. Events, places, names, and characters are either products of the author's imagination or used fictitiously. Any similarity to real persons, living or dead, is coincidental and not intended by the author.

ISBN-13: 979-8-9862236-0-5

Cover design by: Hannah Linder Designs

For Mom,
for always believing,
and for countless sinkfuls of dishes done
while I was squirrelled away writing, oblivious.

The voice of my beloved!
behold, he cometh leaping upon the mountains,
skipping upon the hills.. . .
My beloved spake, and said unto me,
Rise up, my love, my fair one, and come away.

SONG OF SONGS 2:8, 10

The Highwayman

The text of this story previously appeared in *The Most Eligible Bachelor Collection* by Barbour Publishing and as part of *To Catch a Bachelor* by Winged Publications. It has since been modified and updated.

To my darling family,
who remain the lifeblood of my inspiration.

Acknowledgments

My thanks to Lisa K. Jilliani, Charlotte historian and living history interpreter, for the copy of the William Alexander diary, which first introduced me to the life of a colonial wagonmaster. Also to the lovely Liste Members of the now-defunct 18cLife Yahoo group, especially Robert Sherman, living history interpreter at Middleton Place of Charleston, SC, for patiently answering questions about colonial-era men's boots and handling teams of oxen. As always, I uncovered a wealth of information I was barely able to tap in the course of one small story.

My deepest thanks to the Lord, who shuts doors but also opens them. And to my first readers and critique partners. . .both those who loved the story and those who didn't. You all serve a very important purpose in my life!

Chapter 1

The Great Wagon Road, lower Shenandoah Valley, on the eve of the American Revolution

"I can't do this anymore."

Samuel Wheeler said the words so quietly, he wasn't sure his cousin Jedidiah heard him over the patter of rain and the creak and rattle of wagon and harness.

But Jed's ears were sharp. "What do you mean? We have to make this run. All the way to Philadelphia and back, by the end of the month."

The oxen foundered in a patch of mud. "Get up," Sam called, tapping them with the slender goad he always carried, and they forged ahead.

"And," his cousin said, "you can't avoid seeing Sally again. As if you'd want to."

Sam gritted his teeth.

"Of course, if you mean you can't keep silent any longer about your feelings for Sally," Jed went on, all reasonableness, "that's a good thing."

"You know very well what I mean."

Hunched against the rain, Jed snorted. "Ah. That."

"'Tis ridiculous."

"'Tisn't."

"You are to blame for the entire thing."

Jed chuckled. "You put on the coat and boots. Tied the kerchief around your face."

Sam swallowed back a burn. "At your instigation. It was

mad."

"Ah, come now. Admit you've enjoyed it." Jed grinned. "You picked up the whip and stood down tyranny. Put those redcoats on the run, muskets or nay. And they can't find a shred of the one who did it, though his exploits are told all up and down the Great Road."

The familiar elation rose within Sam, but he held onto his grump. "I get no sleep to speak of."

"You slept well enough last night."

"Aye, one whole night in three."

"Stop bellyaching already. Besides, it's tonight you'll see Sally again."

Sam backhanded his cousin's shoulder, and Jed laughed, swaying away. "If we get there in time," Sam said.

"Oh, we will, rain or nay. Nero and Brutus are solid enough, aren't you, boys?"

It wasn't just the oxen. Sam eyed the trickling runoff in the wagon ruts ahead of the trusty pair. If a wheel or yoke didn't break—they'd had that happen often enough, to be sure. He peered up at the low-slung clouds, draping the treetops that pattered with the drips and obscuring the rolling mountains above. Nothing overly threatening there, although one could never tell.

"In all seriousness, though." Jed elbowed him. "When will you finally speak to Sally? It's killing me to watch you make calf-eyes at her and never say a word."

An image of her face rose before Sam—deep brown eyes, flame-red hair peeking from beneath her cap, small white teeth flashing with laughter as she navigated tables at her father's inn, a jaunty chin with a tiny cleft. Freckles scattered across cheeks too thin for beauty, some might say—but she carried more light and joy in her little finger than he possessed in his whole being.

A light and joy that drew him, moth to a flame, till he burned with a longing he could not douse, scorching hotter with each trip up the Great Road and back. But every time he found himself near her, his tongue grew thick in his mouth, his breathing difficult, his hands and feet clumsy. Speaking was out of the question.

Speaking his heart, unthinkable.

What did he have to offer her, after all? She was Sarah Brewster, called Tall Sally of the Lower Valley by some, daughter of the best-kept inn along the Shenandoah. Responsible for a good part of that keeping, herself. He was but an apprentice wagonmaster who made the run from his home in Charlotte Towne to Philadelphia, beholden to his uncle since childhood.

He had nothing. Might always have nothing.

Beside him, Jed snorted. "And still you say naught. Cousin, you'll die a lonely old man if you don't change your ways."

"I can't change who I am," Sam muttered.

"Can't you?" Jed shot him a smug little smile. "You put on the Highwayman costume—aye, at my behest, but you wear it. Redcoats and Tories alike shake in their boots because of you. What is one slip of a girl?"

The girl I love, Sam wanted to say, but he'd not admit that to Jed. His cousin would never let him hear the end of it.

And this Highwayman business complicated everything. He could be shot, for heaven's sake. At the least, found out. It wasn't like such a severely out-of-fashion coat didn't mark him, or the boots—

'Twas the boots that started it all.

~*~*~*~

"Sally, where are the fresh linens?"

Her mother's voice carried from the great room to the kitchen, near the back of the first floor. Shaking her head, Sally kept kneading, quarter turn, fold, push, not missing a beat. "On the table near the counter," she called out. Then more softly, "Right where I told you, Mama."

A pang of guilt assailed her. 'Twasn't Mama's fault she was so beleaguered. Not when Jacky, already not a strong child, suffered a fever three days straight, and in the meantime his twin Johnny got into enough mischief for the two of them. As if he sensed the seriousness of their little brother's illness and poured all his worry into making trouble.

She tucked the bread dough into a stoneware bowl, covered it with a towel, and set it in a corner of the sideboard. It would rise and be ready to bake by morning.

"Sally." Mama came around the corner, her plump, pretty cheeks flushed with exertion. A quick smile flashed despite the last few days' worry, then faded. "I may need you to fetch the doctor for Jacky. I do not like the look of his fever today."

Sally nodded. "Let me know when."

It gave her a reason to call on her older sister, married to the blacksmith, with a pair of children of her own. Polly was small and round and pretty in the same way as Mama, making Sally feel scrawny and awkward by comparison—but she loved Polly dearly and still missed her daily company.

"Later. For now, go count how many rooms remain empty upstairs. We may have unexpected guests on such a wet night."

They'd had many such guests. Sometimes the good

weather brought them, as people traveled harder and farther, but others pressed on despite the rain. These were especially grateful for a warm fire and a hot meal.

Well, the inn was ready.

She whisked away to do as Mama asked, and while she was upstairs, the rattle of a wagon outside came to her ears. She peeked out the window at the end of the hall. It looked to be the Wheeler boys, from Charlotte Towne. On their way up, if she remembered aright. Papa kept track of such things, and she should as well.

Task finished, she lifted her skirts and ran down the stairs, slowing just before reaching the bottom. Then back to the kitchen—yes, the stew and cornbread were ready. A good thing, too, for the Wheeler boys owned hearty appetites.

She hesitated in dishing it up—no telling how long it might take them to unyoke and stable the oxen and linger to talk with Father outside. So she kept herself busy with other things until she heard boots stamping at the back door. Johnny's voice rose above the lower rumble of older male voices. "Any new reports of the Highwayman, Jed?"

Sally stifled a groan. That lad was obsessed with tales of the vigilante.

And of course Jed Wheeler indulged him. "Well, now, I just might. Let me think. . ."

The sound of their tromping covered his words as they made their way into the great room. Sally shook her head, ladling stew into stoneware bowls. As if it weren't bad enough that every time a new tale made its way up the Road—or down—the other village girls were all atwitter. Not that such a figure wasn't romantic enough, of course, but—such a man would never look twice at her, not with all the others to pick from.

Especially not when someone more staid and plain never looked twice at her, either. But she was too sensible to care a fig for that.

She arranged the bowls on a tray, slid in a plate of still-steaming cornbread, added spoons and a generous pat of butter. One last moment to smooth her apron and kerchief—even a sensible girl had her vanity, after all—and then she picked up the tray and sailed into the great room.

Jed and Sam had already found seats at their favorite table, hats off and hanging on the wall, with Johnny's lean form draped over a chair facing them, his boyish face rapt. His back to Sally, Jed gestured wildly with both hands as he talked in that loud, brash voice of his.

Sam, as always, sat quietly next to his cousin, broad face placid and unmoving. He glanced up at Sally's entrance, blue eyes meeting hers and widening a fraction before he nodded once and looked away.

Aye. Like that.

She pasted on a smile and kept walking.

"And then—the sheriff himself showed up to clap irons on the pair. The Highwayman had triumphed yet again, without ever firing a shot. Oh—hullo, Sally! Mm, what do you have for us tonight?"

She set the tray on the table and unloaded it. "Oh, just our usual stew and corncakes." A laugh bubbled—sparked by Jed's infectious grin, she was sure—but other than a flicker from Sam, no response came from that quarter. She ignored the leadenness of her heart and set the empty tray against her hip. "So where are you boys off to this time?"

"Lancaster, then Philly," Jed answered, jovial as you please.

"Any mishaps on the way, so far?"

"None. It's been as fine a trip as we could ask for, apart

from the rain."

Mama bustled in, carrying a pitcher and two tankards. "Gracious, Sally, serving the food before drink! Here you are, boys. Watered ale, our best for you, as always."

Sally murmured an apology and stepped back, face burning. But Sam was head down, spooning his stew. He likely hadn't even noticed Mama's chiding her in front of guests.

Please notice. Please look up. Please look—at me.

But he did not.

Jed, already diverted, slurped from his tankard, shoveling in the stew and launching into another tale for Johnny. And she had work to do.

Chapter 2

The rain stopped and the night warmed, leaving a damp fog to shift through the trees and town. Sally let her shawl sag around her elbows and dangled her basket from her fingertips as she drew a lungful of moist air. Ahh, honeysuckle. One of the loveliest fragrances ever.

The clouds covered the moon, but she knew well the path from her sister's house on the other side of town, where she'd gone after delivering Mama's summons for the doctor. She should have been home by now, but she and Polly had gone to talking, and time slipped away.

With only the Wheeler boys lodging tonight, it wasn't as if Mama needed her overmuch, anyway. They were always among the easiest of guests.

She'd just reached the edge of her father's orchard, which lay behind the barn and pens, when the singing of tree frogs and various insects gave way to the stamp of booted feet and muted sniggering under the trees. A lantern flashed, then dimmed. "Well," a male voice drawled, "if it isn't Tall Sally of the Valley. Come give us a kiss, sweeting."

Lord in heaven, have mercy—it was Willie Brown and his cronies. And not a quarter mile from home.

She kept walking, despite the sudden chill, and gripped her basket and shawl more closely.

"What's the matter, love? Feeling shy tonight?"

A burst of guffaws split the air, and four or five shadows broke from the trees, surrounding her. Slivers of light escaped the lantern, which swung from the hand of one.

She was well and truly caught. Sally clutched her basket but stood as straight as she could. If the blackguard wanted to twit her about her height, well then, she'd use every inch God gave her. "Aren't you cunning, lurking in the dark to trouble women and children. But don't think I don't know who you are."

"And what does it matter? You're naught but a tavern maid."

She held herself still, schooling her features as well as her body. She absolutely would not be intimidated by this bully of a magistrate's son. "You know the Scripture as well as I. 'Be sure your sin will find you out.' 'Twill catch up with you, sooner or late."

Amidst the laughter of the others, Willie leaned toward her, leering under the hat brim pulled low to hide his identity. "My sin can begin finding me out here and now, then. Come, Tall Sally, just a kiss."

"You, sir," she gritted out, "may go to the devil."

One of the ruffians lunged and tore the basket from her grasp. Two others shoved her back and forth between them, and despite her resolve not to, she cried out.

And then she fetched up hard against their leader, who gripped her upper arms. His breath was hot upon her cheek and smelled of strong drink.

"Unhand me! I don't care who you are." She kicked and fought, to no avail, as he laughed, landing rough kisses on her neck and shoulders.

God, forgive me, I should pray for his salvation, but—

"The lady said, unhand her!"

The voice boomed from the edge of the orchard. Willie Brown twitched, but did not release Sally. "Begone, unless you wish for trouble this night."

"'Tis you who begs trouble," the unknown voice said, lower, but no less menacing, "if you do not release the lady and go on your way."

"Indeed?"

Sally thought she'd use the moment to kick Willie in the shins, but he evaded her, keeping hold of her wrists while craning his neck to look. Curiosity got the better of her, and she peeked as well. The shadowy figure of a man in a plumed, cocked hat, and a coat with skirts too long and full to be currently fashionable, was all she could make out.

"For the last time," he said, "release her. Or pay the consequences."

He lifted his arm and shook out—was that the lash of a whip?

One of Willie's cronies swore and fumbled for his pistol, but faster than the eye, the mysterious man's arm flicked. A length of braided leather wrapped around the other man's wrist. Howling, he staggered away, divested of his weapon.

With a yell, the others leaped into action, but one terrible crack came after another, each accompanied by a cry or a flurry of curses.

"And now, you!"

Willie Brown growled and swung Sally about until she was pinned from behind to his chest, one arm around her waist and the other around her neck. "Will you have the lady suffer your lash?"

The shadowy figure did not move as Willie inched backwards, taking Sally with him. In desperation, she sought purchase on his arms with her nails, her teeth—ugh, his fine linen tasted nasty—and again with the heel of her shoe. He cursed but held her more tightly. At their feet, someone moaned. "It's the Highwayman!"

A second dragged himself from the ground. "Not here. He was last seen in Salem—"

The whip licked out again and, catching him by the leg, yanked him off his feet. "It is, and I am here," the man said. "You! Brigands, all. How dare you prey on those weaker than yourselves. How can you call yourselves men?"

Still Sally was pulled backwards. She could not breathe—

With another stroke, he pulled a third man down, accompanied by yet another satisfying howl. Willie hauled her around and made a run for it, but with a crack, they both went tumbling. For a moment the weight of his body crushed her to the earth, then was gone.

"Get out of here, serpent," came that voice, no less terrible than his whip. "Go back to your den."

A last fall of the lash, and Willie fled, his breath coming in gasps like sobs.

Then there was only silence, filled by the pounding of Sally's own heart as she huddled, half afraid to move.

~*~*~*~

He'd just rescued Sally. His Sally.

Sam dared not move at first, after the ruffians had scattered. "Lady, are you hurt?"

A motion—the shaking of her head?—and a tiny "Nay," breathless. But she did not get up.

He took a step toward her, but with a gasp she scrambled away a length or two. The lantern lay on its side a few feet off, and she reached for it.

"Pray, do you leave it shuttered," he said. "But set it upright. Best to not set the forest ablaze."

Still seated, she gazed at him through the darkness. He

could make nothing of her expression in the shadows. “Why? Are you also a brigand?”

A laugh forced its way up out of him. “Nay. Not a gentleman, but not a blackguard either.”

“Are you truly the one they call the Highwayman?”

“That I am, lady.” Ah—what if she recognized his voice? But it was so easy talking to her like this.

He extended a hand. “Might I assist you in getting up?”

She hesitated, then put her hand in his. Light and soft it was, but strong, as she gripped him and hoisted herself to her feet. The extra momentum he put into the motion brought her close to him, close enough to make out the cleft of her chin and the parting of her lips, to smell the marigold and rosemary that was part of her natural fragrance.

Close enough, she might recognize him as well, despite the black silk masking his upper face.

He released her and retreated a step. While she brushed out her skirts and rearranged her clothing, he rolled up the whip, still watching her.

“Have you seen my basket?” she asked, breathless again, not meeting his eye.

He scooped it from the ground and handed it to her. Thanking him, she accepted it and felt inside. With a huff, she turned her search to the ground. “Blasted, unmannerly, unprincipled. . .”

“Are they in the habit of this misbehavior?” he asked.

She paused to glance his way. “Aye. But it’ll do no good to register a complaint. Willie Brown, their leader, is the youngest son of the chief justice. Recently home from his education abroad and weary of life on the frontier, I expect. His father thinks him incapable of wrong. Word has it his father is under pay of the Crown to subvert what he feels is merely colonial justice.”

Unsurprising, that. It was the state of things all up and down the colonies. Worst in the Carolinas, perhaps, but even here—

He spied an item that must have come from her basket and bent to pick it up. She reached at the same time, and their hands met. They both froze before he let her take it. "My pardon," he said, as she said, "Excuse me."

They stood facing each other, her dark gaze regarding him with an intentness he was sure would penetrate his disguise.

Did he care?

Should he care?

"Who are you?" she asked softly.

He gave the breath of a laugh. "No one of consequence."

Her lips pressed firm as she continued to eye him. "I doubt that heartily."

Oh my lady, if you only knew. . .

But he wasn't yet willing to give up this glorious freedom. "And what of yourself, lady? Who do I have the pleasure of addressing this fine evening?"

She snorted, but her mouth curved a little. "I am Sarah—Sally—Brewster. My father is the keeper of Brewster's Inn, just through the orchard."

An answering grin tugged at his mouth at the slight quaver in her voice. He swept her a low bow. "It is an honor, Lady Sarah."

"Oh. Psh." She giggled. "I'm no lady, of a certain."

Sally, reduced to simpering? He didn't know whether to be ashamed or entranced. Perhaps both. "Fetchingly lovely, regardless."

Her breath caught, and she swayed back a little. "Oh—nay. Not I. Too tall, I am, and too thin—"

"Who told you that?" he said. Too quickly. He

suppressed a wince.

Absolutely still, she stared at him, eyes wide. "Wh-why, everyone."

Nay. Not everyone. "Well." He reached out a hand again, and hesitantly, she laid hers in it. His head went swimmy from the touch. "You should not pay attention to those who are only jealous of your radiance." And he bent and brushed a kiss upon the back of her hand.

Sweet heaven. He could stand here all night, just breathing her in.

A tremor coursed through her, and what sounded suspiciously like another soft gasp. Could he truly affect her as deeply as she did him? She tried to tug her hand away, but he held on and straightened, meeting her gaze.

"I—must not detain you any longer," she murmured.

"On the contrary. I should not keep *you* here." But still he did not release her.

She was trembling in earnest now. Fear, or—

"You are still called the Highwayman," she said, in a rush. "Do you mean to rob me as well, now that the others are gone?"

The first inkling of a mad idea seized him. "Nay. Aye. I will take a small token from you, sweet lady—"

And he reeled her toward him, savoring her lithe softness for just the moment as he swooped in to claim her lips. A heartbeat—two—three—

He released her and stepped back, sweeping another bow. "Adieu, fair maiden."

Chapter 3

There was no way a girl could sleep after such a thing.

Snatching up the lantern, clutching her basket, Sally hitched her skirts and ran all the way back to the inn. Inside, she slipped off her shoes and tiptoed to her room on the upper floor, keeping to the sides of the stairs so they wouldn't creak and give her away. A candle still burned in her brothers' chamber, and a glance inside revealed Mama, hands folded and eyes closed, in the rocking chair at the bedside. Sally's heart contracted. If Jacky perished of the fever, as her little sister had—

She pushed aside the thought and hurried upstairs. There, at last, she could catch her breath and let unfurl the memory of the night's adventure.

Adventure. Aye, Johnny would think it such. The Highwayman, indeed! Sally pressed her trembling fingertips to her mouth. Madness it was, that after Willie Brown's rough ministrations, she couldn't find the pluck to defend herself against her outlandishly attired rescuer. What ailed her? Disarmed by a courtly manner and pretty words—oh, she was no better than any other girl in town.

Even if he did soothe the fears Willie Brown and his boys had inspired.

With a huff, she flung her shawl across the foot of the bed then yanked off cap and handkerchief as if they offended her. The pins holding together the front of her gown came next—her fingers fumbled and she dropped one, which obligated her to kneel and feel about until she'd found it.

The angle of his head in the shadows, the slow, graceful way he'd offered his hand—the calloused strength of his grip as he helped her to her feet—the catch of his breath as he'd fetched her close—

She slapped the pile of pins down on her dressing table, ignoring the prick against her hand. Her throat clogged with senseless tears as she wiggled out of the gown then tugged petticoat ties loose.

God—oh God—

She could find no words to finish the prayer. She should be thankful, truly, that Willie and his boys had met their match tonight.

And I do thank You for that, I do, it is only—ah, Lord—

He'd kissed her, for heaven's sake! Why on earth would he do such a thing? It wasn't as if she were pretty, not like other girls—

Who told you that? came his rebuke, as clear as if he stood at her shoulder.

Her petticoat fell around her ankles, and she kicked it across the room. Why would he say such things, if not to take advantage of her? Were all men truly alike, seeking to have their way, either by force or by sweetness?

Because that kiss—and his arms around her for that moment—had left her near to swooning when he retreated into the darkness.

The knot in her stays laces defied her fevered tugging. Sally sank to the edge of the bed and covered her face in her hands. She needed to put this out of her mind. She was far too sensible to fall prey to the flattery of some shadowy, masked rescuer.

If only she could so easily forget the velvet press of his lips against hers.

~*~*~*~

There was no way a man could sleep after all that.

After leaving Sally, Sam hung back in the darkness as she finished gathering her things and hurried home. From the shelter of the orchard, he waited until she went inside, then lingered until the lantern flickered from the attic window he knew was hers. The next hour or so he spent circling the inn and slipping through the adjoining town, just in case the unruly gang decided to make a reappearance. The indignation over finding Sally in danger still burned in his veins, doubly fired by the elation of actually conversing with her.

Not to mention that stolen kiss.

He returned to the inn and for a long time just stood in shadow at the edge of the orchard, watching and listening. When the weariness swept in at last, he made his way to the wagon under cover of shadow and set about removing the disguise.

He tossed his hat onto the seat and followed it with the black silk handkerchief he used as a mask. The coat he threw over the side of the wagon before giving attention to his boots.

Those went first into the small chest he kept stowed under the wagon seat. The boots, like the coat, were too old to be fashionable, but something appealed to him about the softness of the leather and the way the tops hung in a deep cuff when not lashed over his knees. They reminded him of cavalry boots, except the tops were the same supple leather as the shaft.

Sam folded the coat in over the boots, smoothing the long, full skirts, careful not to snag the fantastic embroidery with his roughened fingertips. Some nobleman had once worn the ensemble, he was sure.

More than a year ago he'd been paid to take the chest from Philly down to Salem, only to find the recipient had died. Inquiries yielded no word of any heirs, certainly no one willing to take the thing off his hands.

He and Jed had debated long and hotly before striking off the lock and peering inside. The hat appeared interesting enough, plain black felt cocked on three sides with black braid trim and a black ostrich feather, but then came that coat and the boots after. Lured by the feel of such soft, quality leather, Sam could not resist trying on the boots, on the spot. They fit as if made for him.

Jed, laughing, suggested he don the coat next. Shaking his head, Sam did, feeling foolish but enjoying the lark.

And then, like tonight, there came a cry, an unmistakable sound of someone in distress. Without a word, Sam grabbed the plumed hat and reached for the long whip he'd always taken just a little too much pride in, then ran to see what was the matter. Only as an afterthought did he pull up the kerchief he kept tied about his neck, covering the lower half of his face.

A lark, he told himself. That first time was a simple matter of a pickpocket, quickly dispatched with but a flick or two of his whip. The woman Sam rescued was so grateful, and the notoriety afterwards went quite to his head, that he and Jed plotted more. Once in Philadelphia, to challenge a group of redcoats. Another time in Winchester, where Tories harassed a man who voiced his discontent with the crown. Two or three in Big Lick—none of those planned—but Sam had gotten skilled at putting on the disguise quickly and had cut eye holes in the kerchief, to tie it over his head and conceal his identity.

Dozens of times, up and down the Great Road. Indeed, it had gotten quite out of hand.

Inside the inn, he slipped off his boots and crept up the stairs to the chamber he shared with Jed. Nearly always the same room, just below Sally's.

Jed snored then rolled over, and Sam stretched out beside him. He lay for a moment listening. Nothing but the usual creaks and whispers of a house. Lord willing, Sally was asleep long ago.

Lord, please let her not lose sleep over this night.

The next he knew, it was full daylight, and Jed was gone.

Memory of the night before returned in a rush. Pulse racing, Sam rose, splashed water on his face and smoothed back his hair without bothering to retie it, then grabbed his boots and headed downstairs.

A feminine voice floated up the stairs to him—Sally? No, her mother. He paused at the bottom step. Snuffling came from the direction of the kitchen. Softly, he crept down the hall to peer around the corner.

Sally stood at a table, back to him, stirring something in a bowl, but slowly. She stopped, her shoulders lifting and falling with a sigh, and one hand came up to swipe across her eyes.

His heart seized. Sally, crying? Had he done that, or—

Please, Lord, if You will, let her brother be well!

"Sally? Is aught amiss?"

His own voice startled him, and she spun with a gasp. Shadows rimmed her eyes, and aye, she'd been weeping. "Oh—I—nay, all is well."

He let himself relax but a little. "Your brother?"

Another sniffle, but she waved her hand. "He's better this morning, thankfully."

"Ah." He stood there, stupidly. *Come on, man! Find your tongue again.*

A scowl marred Sally's fine brow. "You're up late, aren't you? Breakfast is in the great room, if your cousin hasn't eaten it all—"

"Ah, Sam! There you are," came Jed's booming voice.

Sam gritted his teeth. Should he thank his cousin for the interruption, or pummel him?

It was more words than she'd ever heard at one time from the quiet wagonmaster—and he couldn't have picked a worse time. Catching her mooning and blubbering over a bowl of blackberries, when she should have had the pies baking already.

Just for a second, though, he'd nearly caused her heart to stop, and for the most unaccountable reason. . .

She glanced away as Sam's blustering cousin clapped him on the shoulder. "Late to rise again, I see! How many times have I told you to lay off the drink?"

Sally shot them both a sharp glance. Sam looked—what *was* that look? His head dropped, a single blond lock sweeping across a jaw gone completely crimson.

Something in her sank. "Where did you get drink? My father doesn't like to serve anything stronger than watered ale, unless someone's dying."

Jed turned a too-wide grin on her. "Oh, Sam keeps a store in the wagon. Don't you, Sam?"

Why was he so cheerful about it? Men. Bumbling clods, all.

With the possible exception of one. . .

She turned away. It hurt to breathe. "Begone, both of

you. I have work to do."

The hallway door to the outside slammed, and Johnny's voice overlaid the patter of his running feet. "Jed! Sam! You'll never guess! The Highwayman was here last night. In our town!"

Sally knees nearly buckled. *Sweet Lord, have mercy.* Word was out already?

Sam could feel his face blanch, and the sudden weight of Jed's gaze upon him. "Was he, now?" his cousin drawled. But it was Sally who consumed all his attention—Sally, gripping the table as if her life depended on it, her own face gone pale.

Johnny was still jumping up and down. "Sally, did you hear? The Highwayman!"

"I hear," she said, faintly.

The lad turned his grin upon Jed. "The chief justice is mad as a wet hen because he said the Highwayman accosted his son last night—but everyone knows that Willie Brown is nothing but trouble. Him and his boys—"

"Hold your tongue!"

The crackle of Sally's voice yanked them all to attention, her dark eyes wide and more shadowed than before. Sam's hands twitched with the sudden need to catch her close.

"Do you wish to get us all in trouble?" Sally went on, her voice lower. "It's bad enough Willie Brown and the others run wild as they do, but this—"

Johnny and Jed gaped at her, but Sam did not move. Johnny said, "Well, the magistrate is fit to be tied. Swears he'll catch the Highwayman once and for all—"

Fire crawled up Sam's spine.

Sally reached behind her for a chair, and without thinking, Sam whisked one into place. She glanced up, her eyes glazed with distress, and murmured her thanks.

Her gaze found Johnny again. "What do they say happened?"

He could fix this. He could—

Nay. He should go. Now. Before his presence caught them all in the magistrate's sights.

"Willie and his boys, they said the Highwayman challenged them. That they was minding their own business, and he stepped out and took to callin' them names—"

Jed's gaze was like to bore a hole in Sam. He backed out of the kitchen, taking a better grip on his boots and seizing Jed's arm. Jed startled as if just now coming awake. "Pardon, Sally, but we're long past needing to be on our way. Thank you kindly for breakfast."

Who dragged who down the hallway to the great room was hard to say. They stumbled over each other at the edge of the buffet and, after a quick glance to make sure they were alone, Jed gave Sam a hard glare. "What in heaven's name did you do last night?"

But Sam was hauling on his boots and pulling a spare cloth from his breeches pocket to wrap up a hasty breakfast from the buffet. Hanged if he'd answer that before being well away from here.

Chapter 4

She needed to compose herself. She *had* to.

But she stayed rooted to the chair, apron over her face.

She'd thought the affair over with when the Highwayman had chased the last of her attackers into the night. But it had just begun. *You're naught but a tavern wench.* If Magistrate Brown was after the Highwayman in all this, Willie would make sure she suffered as well. Was there anyone within reach who could stop this madness?

"Lord God," she choked, "oh God, help me." A new fear lashed at her. "And help—help the Highwayman, whoever he is."

Now where had that come from? Praying for someone she didn't even know, who had played on her girlish affections as surely as Willie sought to take advantage. Yet, she couldn't shake the conviction that he needed the prayer.

Wherever he was.

"Sally! Whatever ails you?"

She startled upright, hastily uncovering her face and wiping her tears at Mama's concerned inquiry. "'Tis naught. Truly."

Mama gave her a long look. "Well. See that you finish the pie in time for luncheon, then."

"Aye, Mama."

She settled herself at the table's edge once more, surveying the bowl of sweetened berries, the sack of flour, the rolled-out pie crust at the ready. She should put the crust in the pie dish, first—

"Sweetheart? Is all well?"

Her father this time. She clapped a hand over her heart. "Papa! Have a care in startling people."

He smiled, but his dark eyes still shone with concern, as Mama's had. And rather than leaving quickly, he took a step forward. "And I ask again, are you well?"

She straightened, wiping her hands on her apron. "Of—of course, Papa."

He peered into her face, his broad features calm. "Jed and Sam left just now."

"Aye." Where was he going with this? She flicked a hand. "They were late getting on their way. Sam—slept too long."

She swallowed past a sudden burn at the reminder that quiet, dependable Sam was secretly a drunkard.

"Well. It's interesting, that. Before he left, young Sam asked me to tell you not to believe anything ill you might hear about him." Her father's gaze became uncommonly sharp. "What would you know about that?"

Sally swayed a little. Her thoughts were a perfectly clean slate. "I have no idea."

"So, you know naught about whether the lad harbors some secret affection for you?"

"Sam? Nay!" But even as she said it, she could see again the deep flush that stained his face at Jed's jibe over the drink.

The little smile was back on Papa's face. "Nay?" But when she only stared at him, his expression faded into sadness. "You're nearly twenty, sweet girl. I know you don't want to be working for your papa forever, that you need a home and family of your own—"

"I'm happy here," she protested, but his hand brushed her elbow, and the smile returned, more tender this time.

"Shh, daughter. I'll not be offended if you admit you long for a bit more than this." He started to turn away and hesitated. "And Sam is a good lad. If he ever finds the pluck to speak his mind, you should listen."

If Sam ever—? Nay. Last night, Sam hardly spared her a look. Men were distractible creatures, true, especially where their feed was concerned, but—nay.

Besides, last night—

"Papa?"

Her father stopped at the doorway and glanced back.

"Papa." Sally clutched her apron then forced herself to smooth the fabric against her skirt. "There is something I must tell you."

He turned, waiting.

She took a breath, plunged on before she could lose the moment. "The Highwayman's appearance, last night. He—he defended me, from Willie Brown and his cronies."

Papa's gaze narrowed, and his mouth hardened.

"After taking word to the doctor that Mama needed him for Jacky, I stopped at Polly's. And lingered, when I shouldn't have, but—I was nearly home when Willie and his boys stopped me."

"Were you harmed?" he asked, in a quiet, dangerous voice she'd never heard.

"N-nay."

"Thank the good Lord for that!"

She bobbed a nod. "But, I might have been, if—if he had not come." She swallowed. "I do not know why he was there, but I was grateful."

"As well you should be." He rubbed a hand across his mouth and jaw. "Did he behave honorably?"

"Aye."

The answer was out before she could stop it. Why did

she feel the need to defend him?

Papa moved at last, nodding and shifting away to stare at the floor, smoothing back his iron-grey hair tied in a neat queue.

Her hands knotted in her apron again. "Should we—can we—inform someone? I know Magistrate Brown doesn't have the facts aright. . ."

"At present, there's none other to appeal to," Papa said. "Let me think on this. And pray. It may be—blast it all, anyway." He shot her another dark look. "Stay close to the inn for now. If we need aught, I'll send Johnny or Jacky. Understand me?"

She gave a mute nod, her mouth dry again.

"Thank you for telling me, sweet girl. It would break my heart if aught happened to you."

And then he was gone.

She went back to the table and blew out a breath. Her mind was quite in disarray now, but her hands knew the task of pie making well enough—

A flutter of white on the windowsill—across the room, above another worktable—caught her eye. She frowned. What was that? It looked like a folded paper, but she could not remember anyone leaving anything there.

She crossed the room, reached for it, unfolded it to reveal an attempt at an elegant hand—she could tell for how sloppy it was—written with many scrolls and flourishes. Then the wording made itself clear, and her breath caught.

May I call on you one evening? Not tonight, but soon. Look for me by moonlight.

~The Highwayman

~*~*~*~

The morning started fine enough, rounded mountaintops shimmering against the sky and birds twittering in the clear daylight, but now the blazing sun set Sam's head to pounding as he trudged beside the wagon. And a sickness swirled in his gut the farther they got from Brewster's.

With every step, he was sure they shouldn't have left.

He tipped his head to squint upward, from under the brim of his plain black hat. Nearly midday. He was used to delays, but this was ridiculous. "Are you sure this track leads back to the Great Road?" he asked Jed, who walked ahead of the team.

When they'd tried to leave town, they discovered the magistrate had men stationed both north and south on the Great Road, searching wagons and saddlebags in his effort to find the Highwayman.

"The hostler said so. Down past the mill, up along the creek, over the hill."

"'Twas an hour ago."

"If you hadn't been so slow in starting—" Jed scowled. "Why in the world did you run off? And what was so important to discuss with Mr. Brewster?"

"Last trip to the necessary," Sam said. It wasn't completely untrue.

But he couldn't explain any of it, yet. Not his sudden need to have the goodwill of Sally's father, nor that other small task he'd decided to carry out before they left. Would Sally even find the note before someone else did?

Better that she not expect to see him again. For her, and for him.

Lord, I believe I've made an awful mess of this.

"I thought you didn't want to do this anymore?" Jed said.

"I don't. Didn't." Sam swallowed his rising bile. "You know how it is, I hear something, and then—I can't stand by and do nothing." He chewed the inside of his cheek for a moment. "This time, it turned out to be Sally."

The annoyance in Jed's expression bled to shock.

"Apparently these local boys, led by the chief justice's son, have a habit of causing trouble. They were—well, I couldn't let them lay hands on her like that."

"Good Lord."

"That He is."

Jed laughed shortly.

"We shouldn't have left so fast," Sam went on.

Jed did turn on him at that, stepping out of the way of the team. "You'd rather have those boys search our wagon? We have to finish this run and get home."

"Nay."

But when the magistrate's men didn't find the Highwayman. . .what then? What about Sally and her family?

Oh, Lord.

"So." Jed shot him a sidelong look. "After you rescued Sally, what happened? Did she run straight home, or did you talk to her?"

Despite his best efforts, a grin tugged at Sam's mouth. The sick feeling disappeared for just a moment at the memory of Sally in his arms. "That, cousin, would be none of your business."

Jed's hooting laughter echoed across the pasture.

Chapter 5

Look for me by moonlight.

And what, pray tell, had he meant by that? A moon had waxed and begun to wane, and still the mysterious Highwayman did not make another appearance.

Sally heaved a sigh and, dipping her rag in the bucket of soapy water, went back to scrubbing the table. Not a breath of air stirred in the great room and no one was about, so she'd shed her apron and gown for the work.

She was so weary of the flipping and flopping of her thoughts. The Highwayman. Sam. One who had rescued her. . .kissed her. The other who, at least by Papa's reckoning, was sweet on her. She blew a stray wisp out of her face and scrubbed harder. She'd known Sam since he was a boy, traveling up the Great Road with his uncle and cousins. His uncle, complaining of rheumatism and the need to tend to matters at home, had turned the run over to Sam and Jed, a handful of years before either reached their majority. All she knew of Sam before then was that his parents and young siblings perished in some terrible tragedy, and the uncle had taken him in.

Might be no wonder Sam was grave and quiet. 'Twas better than thinking of him as dull.

Better his dullness, perhaps, than the Highwayman. . .of whom she knew next to nothing. A strong, working-man's grip. A gentle kiss, despite the way he'd pulled her to him. Terrifyingly accurate with the whip. A smile flitted across her lips. No wonder lads and lasses alike were enthralled with tales of him.

He was gallant, she'd give him that. And apparently possessed of a ferociously protective nature.

Still, 'twas hardly enough to know whether she could trust such a man. Whether he was not merely trifling with her, as she steadfastly maintained to her heart.

Her pitifully desperate heart. Sally snorted. Truly, she was no better than any other girl—

"Sally?" Mama's voice was a soft intrusion, but insistent as always. "I believe we are out of orris root. Might you run to the market and fetch some?"

Some of the furor had died over the Highwayman's appearance more than a fortnight ago—at the least, the magistrate gave up guarding the Great Road—but Papa hadn't yet told her how far she might safely venture. Did she dare run to the market and back?

"Aye, Mama."

"And while you're at it, we're a little low on coffee."

Sally nodded and slid back into her blue linen gown. Mama lingered as Sally pinned the front closed and pinned and tied her apron back on, over all. "I don't often tell you, but you've been an invaluable help to me." A sad smile curved Mama's mouth. "Your Papa thinks I've been working you too hard. But I'm grateful you've always been willing, especially when Jacky was sick."

Sally reached for her wide-brimmed straw hat and tied it at her nape. "You're more than welcome, Mama."

Mama handed her a small pouch of coins. "Your Papa said there's a young man who might be interested. . .?"

Sally felt her face go crimson. Her breath seized. *He does not know. . .he cannot know. . .he's thinking only of Sam.* "I—don't know, Mama. He's not spoken." She slipped the pouch through the slit in her skirt and petticoats, into her pocket.

Mama's smile warmed. "How exciting, though."

Sally could almost hear the thoughts of her pretty, plump mother, measuring her angular height and wondering who could possibly want her. "I'll return soon."

She gave Mama a quick peck on the cheek, then made her escape. It was a fine, hot day, but she set a brisk pace, glad to put distance between herself and the inn for a bit.

Though the late afternoon warmth made everyone languid at the market, the dry-goods seller greeted her with a cheery smile. "Tall Sally! We've not seen you in a week or three."

She gave the older man a quick grin in return. "Mama's had me a bit busy. But I'm here today."

"And what is your pleasure this time?"

"Coffee and sugar. And some orris root. Are we still avoiding tea?"

"We are indeed, Miss Brewster, but if your mother has a hankering for it, I have some, properly smuggled and untaxed."

She laughed. "Not this time, Mr. Messer, but I thank you."

While waiting for him to package her items, she lingered over a display of fine china, admiring the gold leaf and delicate rosebuds. She'd just lifted a cup and was examining the underside when a voice rumbled in her ear, "You never did give me that kiss, Tall Sally."

'Twas all she could do to set the cup back down, clattering on its saucer, and not knock the whole display to the floor. One glance told her she was but a hand's breadth from the hated leer of Willie Brown.

She twitched away, putting at least half the floor between them.

Lord. . .oh, Lord. . .

Willie leaned indolently on the counter, clad in a suit of green ditto as if he were going to a fancy dress ball and not merely loitering here in the store. His shoes bore a shine fit to blind the casual eye, his dark hair pulled back into an oh-so-stylish queue, one lock falling across his brow.

For some reason, it made her think of Sam, and his fiery blush when Jed teased him about drinking too much.

"I'm missing a lantern, Tall Sally. You wouldn't happen to know where it went, would you?"

"Of course not," she snapped.

Mr. Messer set her packages on the counter. She made to step around Willie, but he shifted to block her. "I've not forgotten," he said, very low, "the lashing I took for you. You owe me a kiss."

Matching him inch for inch, she lifted her chin and met his gaze. "Should you be speaking to me? I'm naught but a tavern wench, after all."

Once again he sidestepped to halt her progress.

"Willie Brown," said the seller. "No trouble here today, please."

"There's no trouble," Willie drawled. "I'm only paying compliments to one of your customers, but she seems not to appreciate them. How ungenerous of her."

He smiled into her eyes as if daring her to defy him.

She would not budge. Dared not. "I must needs get home, *kind* sir."

The smile widened. "It would be an honor to accompany you."

Her body flushed hot, then cold. *I would rather die!* But she smiled thinly. "Thank you, but I'll not inconvenience you."

"'Tis no inconvenience, Miss Brewster."

At that moment, a double patter of young boys' feet pounded across the steps and into the store. Johnny, leading Jacky, breathless. "Sally! Mama and Papa bid you home. This minute."

Never so relieved for the interference of her brothers, Sally bobbed to Willie, whisked her purchases into her basket, and hurried after the boys.

When they were out of earshot, Jacky said, "Papa found out Mama had sent you to market, and oh, he was vexed. So we came after you."

Johnny shot a glance behind them. "Did we do right? That was Willie Brown talking to you."

"You did indeed." She laughed, swinging her basket like a young girl. "And what do you hear lately of the Highwayman?"

Sam poked a few twigs into the small fire then sat back and surveyed the purple twilight draping the edges of majestic, rolling mountains. On such a clear, cool night, a day's journey south of Winchester for the oxen, he and Jed had decided to camp out.

This was one of his favorite stretches of the Great Road, truth be told. He loved the entire Shenandoah Valley, from above the James River to up past Winchester. Though Charlotte Towne nestled in a pretty enough area, the river valley called to him as few places did.

Maybe that had something to do with why he'd fallen in love with Sally. Or maybe it was Sally who made him love the valley.

Sweet Sally of the river valley.

Was there any hope she'd look at him twice? Perhaps

even entertain his suit?

"So how's it feel to be shot of the Highwayman?" Jed asked. Breaking into his best thoughts, as always.

Sam chewed a thumbnail. "Am I shot of him? Truly?"

Jed laughed. "'Tis been deadly dull without him these past three weeks."

Hanged if he'd admit agreeing with his cousin. "Quiet, it is."

Jed's eyes gleamed as he sat back and propped a forearm on his bent knee. "Thought you didn't care for quiet. There's Sally and all."

Sam just shook his head, and Jed sobered, looking off over the mountaintops. "Appears whatever quiet we might have is soon at an end, anyway. With the way my father has been pestering us to give more time to the militia back home. . .and the Crown's officials have become too bold by half. First it was the Stamp Act, then they renewed the tax on tea. . .now they want to restrict the import of gunpowder? Best we look to our own stores and rifles, no mistake." He picked up a pebble and threw it. "But it might have been fun to be in on the destruction of the tea in Boston, don't you think?"

Despite himself, Sam chuckled. "It might indeed, if we'd been up north at the time."

His cousin grinned again. "Speaking of chucking things, I'm surprised you didn't toss the Highwayman's chest in the river after we left Staunton."

"Tempting, that."

He still could. Except. . .except he'd left Sally a note. All but promised to see her again, and not as himself.

Could he really follow through on that? He wanted to, oh he wanted to. He'd never dreamed how easy it could be to speak with her.

If only he could be sure his intervening that night hadn't caused her and the family more trouble.

A sudden longing to see her rose up and gripped him by the throat.

"How far are we from Brewster's?"

Jed stared at him before a slow smile stole across his face. "You know we're still two days out. Even with fair weather."

He couldn't breathe for a moment for the strength of his need to know she was well.

"I can't get there tonight, even on horseback. . .even if I could get a horse," he heard himself say.

His cousin's grin widened. "You can get one at tomorrow's stop."

An hour or two's fast ride, he could be there by midnight. Perhaps.

Would he be able to rouse Sally and persuade her to come out?

His hands tightened around the stick he held. "What if she hates me when she finds out who I truly am?"

Jed laughed. "What if she doesn't?"

He was the worst kind of fool for even contemplating it.

Chapter 6

Come to me by moonlight. . .

Sally drifted in a dream where the moon hung unnaturally full and bright. A masked rescuer rode a splendid black horse and carried a shining sword, with a pair of pistols strapped to his waist. The horse's hooves beat a steady tattoo on the hardened dirt of the road that ran past the inn, first galloping southward, then north—

She startled awake.

Plink. Plink, plink.

What on earth?

Limbs trembling, she climbed from her bed and peered out the open window. A fat half-moon was just rising above the far trees, and—

At the edge of the stableyard, a shadowy figure stood, garbed in a full-skirted coat and plumed hat.

"Dear Lord in heaven!" It was an honest prayer. What should she do?

While she watched, he tossed something. Another *plink* sounded right next to her, making her flinch, and a pebble rolled across her floor.

She scrambled for her shawl and leaned out the window. He sauntered forward until he stood just below her.

"What are you doing?" she whispered.

"Good evening, lady."

The timbre of his voice sent a shiver through her. *Oh Lord. . .I am such a fool.* "You are mad. Why are you here?"

His chuckle floated to her. "Mad, aye. But I have come to call on you. Did you receive my message?"

She clutched her shawl over her chest as if to keep her heart inside. "I did."

"And? What is your reply?"

"I—" She gulped. "You are mad."

"Aye, you said that once." The laughter rippled through his voice, tugging at her again. "Will you come down?"

"Ah—give me a moment."

She stepped back from the window and looked wildly around. It would be indecent to go out to him in a state of undress, but—oh, there was nothing for it. He'd just have to wait.

Her hands shook so badly she could hardly thread the lacing through the eye of the bodkin, or work the laces properly. It was the worst stays lacing she had ever done.

"This is madness. *I* am mad. Going out there to talk to—oh Lord, help me?"

Her frantic whisper ended on a high-pitched squeak. She tied off the lacing, snatched up a petticoat and stepped into it. She probably had it backwards, but no one would notice in the dark, especially with a bedgown thrown over and a shawl to top it off.

She tiptoed down the stairs, past the boys' room and that of her parents, down and past the kitchen and out the back door. Around the backside of the inn, and—

There, standing in the shadow of the stable.

She looked around. The stableyard was perfectly quiet, but that didn't mean no one else was watching. The moonlight wasn't as bright as it could be, but the lightness of her shawl would give her away.

Ah, well. She gulped a breath and strode across to him.

He met her at the edge of shadow. "You honor me," he

whispered.

She wrapped her shawl more tightly. “Why did you come?” She hadn’t meant to sound accusatory, but—she had to know.

“To see you.” He seemed to hesitate, though his features were completely unreadable with that mask under his hat. “Are you well?”

“I—am.”

“And your family? I was concerned that the magistrate’s whelp and his dogs would trouble you further.”

Oh, she wished she could see his face—and more of his eyes than a muted sparkle. His quiet fierceness warmed her in ways she dared not think about. “Nothing of any significance.”

It would do no good to tell him of the incident at the market.

He gazed steadily at her, as if he could see she was hedging. “Would you tell me if there was trouble?”

She swallowed at the protective growl to his voice. “Why does it matter to you?”

For a moment, he did not move. At last, with a long exhale, he extended a hand. “Walk with me to the orchard, sweet lady? Just under cover of the trees, no farther, I promise.”

With a nervous dip of her head, she put her hand in his, let him lead her.

If only this were real—she so wanted this to be real—

They stepped into full shadow, and he turned to face her, but did not release her hand. “I had to know whether those brigands had returned. And then, of course, there was my note.” He brought her hand to his lips. “I—promised.”

His breath fanned her skin, and she shivered again.

“Are you cold?”

"N-nay."

His thumb brushed across her knuckles, then his lips followed.

Oh, to feel them on hers again. . .

"You are very bold, sir," she managed to get out.

He stopped, slowly straightened, released her hand, and withdrew. "You are right. I should not presume."

Her heart had not ceased its racing. One of the apple trees provided a handy place to sink back against, for support.

She should go. She shouldn't have ventured out here to begin with. Who was he, really, that he made her want to stay?

He wanted to laugh for the sheer joy of standing out here with her, moonlight filtering through the trees, but he forced himself to calm, mimicking her stance and leaning back, facing her. . .letting himself drink her in. She was almost unbearably lovely—the pale oval of her face framed by hair uncovered and braided across her shoulder, her neckline bare above the shawl.

But he had to tread lightly.

From the other side of the orchard, where he'd left it safely tethered in darkness, his horse snorted and stamped. He could just make out the widening of Sally's eyes, then her smile. "A horse, hm? Well, that's never been part of the Highwayman legend."

"Oh?"

She laughed. "I asked my brothers what they could tell me about you. They're quite enamored of your exploits."

"Daft lads." He couldn't douse his grin. "And you don't

share their sentiments?"

Her chin tucked. "I did not—before."

So completely fetching, the way she went all shy on him. "No? That makes you a sensible girl, I expect."

She shot him a glance. Her laugh this time was brittle. "Nay, it makes me dull."

Did she really think so? "I like sensible. And you are anything but dull."

She made a sound, like a hiccup, and turned half away. "Stop. Please."

"What?"

She didn't respond, and when he took a step toward her, she slid further away.

"What is it, sweet Sally?"

She twitched, but did not look at him. "Do not—do not trifle with me. 'Tisn't fair."

His pulse stuttered at the catch in her voice.

"I should not have come out here. I should—"

"Please." The word burst from him. "Do not leave. Not yet."

She hesitated, looked back over her shoulder.

"I would never trifle with you," he said.

For a long moment, neither of them moved, and he hardly breathed—then she eased back into place against the tree. "I want to believe you," she said.

He fought the urge to fidget as she regarded him.

"Why me?" she asked, finally. "You could have your choice of girls all up and down the Great Road."

Could he? The thought had never occurred to him. "I want—a sensible girl. One who doesn't let herself be moved by wild tales."

She chewed her lip. "You're only saying that."

"I am not."

Her eyes widened a little at his vehemence, then narrowed. "Who are you? Truly?"

"I am—" He'd known questions such as this were a possibility. "I am no one. Truly. I was a foundling, and even now I am completely dependent upon others for my livelihood."

Still she studied him. After a long moment, she sniffed. "As are we all. Dependent upon others, that is."

His throat ached. Here was where he had to be honest with her. Prove that he was not merely toying with her affections.

"I have nothing to offer a lovely, sensible girl like yourself. I have nothing to offer any girl. Forgive me for—taking advantage last time we met. You deserve an honest courtship and not—not clandestine meetings at midnight."

"And you could yet be saying that, simply to gain my trust."

A valid point, but what more could he do to show her? One hand went to his hat. He could unmask himself, this moment, and reveal who he was. He should. If he truly loved her—

"Nay." Sally spoke the word quietly, but with force, despite the tremor in her voice. "Don't. Please."

He stopped, peered at her.

She swiped a hand over her eyes. "I know 'tis selfish, but if I don't know who you are. . .they can't force me to tell them."

Oh, sweet lass. He settled the hat back into place. "So there *has* been trouble."

Chapter 7

"Aye." She could hardly keep her voice from shaking, but something about his concern brought it all spilling out of her. "Papa is afraid for me, and says I'm to stay close to the inn. But two days past Mama needed me to go to the market. . .and Willie Brown was there."

He took a step closer, but this time she had no urge to sidle away.

"There was no opportunity for aught but idle threats, but. . ." The breath she drew hurt. "I fear mostly for my family."

"Can no one stand up to him? To the magistrate?"

She lifted a shoulder.

"If—" He wheeled away, pacing back and forth. "If all the men of the town stood together, perhaps. . ."

Sally snorted. "Most men are cowards, truth be told."

He swung toward her, let out a long breath. "Aye. That we are."

"I didn't mean you!"

He shook his head. Another sigh. "Sweet lady, you have no idea."

"But you. . ." How could he think himself so? "You faced all of Willie Brown's gang. And they had pistols. And you've done"—she thought of all that Johnny had told her—"so many things, that no one else dares."

"That is the Highwayman," he murmured.

Words failed her. This strong, dashing man thought himself a coward?

"But ... I still don't understand."

He kept silence so long, fiddling with the deep cuffs of his coat, she wondered if he would answer. Then, "I would explain if I could, but I may not. Yet."

Oh, blast the tiny flame of hope kindling at that one word, *yet.* That meant—it meant he might see her again.

"You plan to tell me, then? At some point?"

His head lifted. Was that a slow smile on his lips? "Aye. I will tell you. I cannot promise how long that might take, however." The smile faded, and he stepped closer. "Dare I hope that you would welcome the prospect of my calling on you again?"

She raised her chin. Sauciness seemed the only proper recourse here. It was that, or fling herself wantonly into his arms. "That, sir, depends upon how you comport yourself."

He gave a breathy laugh. "I shall be the perfect gentleman then."

"I thought you said you were not a gentleman?" She couldn't suppress her own chuckle.

"This time I will ask before I hold your hand. Or kiss you."

Lightning sizzled along her nerves. "Well, that is some comfort, I suppose." She laughed again at the ridiculousness of it, conversing with him like this. "So, how did you become the Highwayman?"

"Oh, my lady." A rueful laugh, a sigh. "Truth be told, it started by accident. . ."

The moon stood overhead before a lull brought Sam to the realization of how long they'd talked. He cast an eye upward from his seat beneath an apple tree. Just a few hours till daylight—and he had one errand yet to see to.

He thought about leaving that until he and Jed were on their way south, but he feared delaying it any longer.

Sally's languid sigh drew him. For that matter, everything she had said and done this night drew him. She sat facing him, braced as before against a tree trunk, head tipped back, eyes closed. "I suppose. . .I should go back, let you ride away to wherever it is you won't tell me you're going."

"Ha." He pushed to his feet, reached out to help her up. "'Tis I who should let you return to your bed. I imagine a day starts early at Brewster's."

There was no hesitation this time when she put her hand in his and swung herself up. Neither did she try to pull away, but stood, studying what she could see of his face in the shadows.

Can you recognize me, Sally? Do you see anything of the man I truly am, beyond this costume?

He wanted her to know, but—as she had said, not yet. Perhaps never, depending upon how badly he'd aroused the magistrate's ire.

Perhaps he could persuade Sally to come south with him to Charlotte Towne. . .

And for what? He hardly earned his own keep in his uncle's household. What did he know that would provide for a wife and, someday, God willing, a family?

Sally had begged him not to trifle with her. Was that not what he'd done, in calling on her, in lingering here?

And yet, he could not bring himself to release her hand. Or, it seemed, to stop his free one from cupping her cheek.

She leaned into his touch, her lashes falling for a moment and lips curving. "I don't even know what to call you."

He caught himself just in time from replying with his name. "Call me—ungentlemanly." He dipped his head and lightly kissed the cleft in her chin. Oh, how long he'd wanted to do that.

With a tiny gasp, she went completely still, but did not withdraw.

He brushed his lips across one cheek, then the other. "A rogue." The tip of her nose, charmingly chilled from the cool of the evening. "A man who has, I fear, fallen most unsensibly in love with you."

Her eyes opened wide. For a moment, time hung suspended, then she stretched to press her mouth to his.

~*~*~*~

Not stolen this time, but given with her whole heart.

Tipping his head to better meet her kiss, he gathered her against him, and she slid one hand around his neck. Oh, she was melting. She'd never dreamed it could feel so right to be in a man's arms—or perhaps it was just the moonlight, the hat and coat, and—the loneliness that tore at her, night after night. He smelled faintly of the cedar scent she'd detected that first time, and of leather and green grass.

They broke, but he pressed his cheek to hers, his breath fanning her neck. "Sweet Sally. I cannot ask you to wait for me, but I will find some way to return to you—either as the Highwayman, or as myself. Before the year is out, good Lord willing."

She could hardly think, let alone respond, except to tighten her arms around him.

"I should have asked if you have any suitors."

"I do not," she whispered. Sam did not count—poor lad, whose suit she might have welcomed, if—

If she were not standing here, being held—and kissed, again—by the one of whom all the wild tales were told. So much for being sensible.

He drew back a little to look at her. "None? At all?"

"None."

He stared at her so long she had to fight to not squirm, but at last he drew her close again, tucking her head to his shoulder. "I am glad of it."

Poor Sam indeed.

Chapter 8

It was selfish of him to be glad she claimed no other suitors, but Sam could not deny the soaring of his heart at her words.

Nor the pounding fury that rose in him at the thought of that blackguard Willie Brown threatening to lay hands on her again.

Which was why a certain chief justice needed to know what kind of cur he'd spawned.

He'd seen Sally safely back inside the inn, but not before a last whispered assurance on her part that she did, indeed, welcome his calling on her again, and a last sweet but regrettably short kiss. Then he'd forced himself to hurry away. He'd already claimed far more from her than he'd a right to.

The magistrate's dwelling was not difficult to find, being the largest and grandest home, on a hillside overlooking the town. Sam tied his horse at the edge of the property and crept forward.

The barking of a hound he silenced with a bit of jerky from his pocket. The stone wall proved no difficulty, either, nor the back entrance to the house.

This was where the line between justice and vengeance blurred. He and Sally had discussed that very question this night—how to draw such lines—as well as many other things. How did he plan to keep this within the proper limits? He did not know.

Inside the main bedchamber, Sam eased back the

draperies around the bed, letting the moonlight illuminate the bulk and features of an older man, flabby but pinched even in sleep. Beside him, an equally portly woman snored.

A woman's presence might complicate matters. But, it could work in his favor as well.

Once he had all the drapes pulled to the bedposts, Sam withdrew to the window, putting the moonlight behind him, and took his whip from the deep pocket of his coat.

"Magistrate Brown," he said, slowly and clearly, "it is time to awake."

A snort and a cough interrupted the snoring. Both sleepers inhaled as if surfacing from the depths of their slumber.

Sam repeated the injunction.

Mistress Brown gave a cry, clutching the bedcovers to her neck, as the magistrate startled and half rolled over, reaching for something beside the bed.

"Don't move, either of you," Sam said. "My whip is faster than your hand, and I'd hate to injure you before I've had my say."

The man froze, his eyes glinting a bit in the dark. "Who are you?"

"Consider me a voice for the people. Word has it that you, as an official of the Crown, are subverting justice for the sake of lining your pockets."

Slowly, the magistrate sat up in bed, his face set in hard lines. Beside him, his wife squeaked again. "Hush, Mary. I'll not let him hurt you."

Sam snorted. "You promise to protect your own wife, but what about wives and daughters of the men under your jurisdiction?"

"Of what nonsense do you speak?"

A wry chuckle escaped Sam. "Your son and his cronies.

Despite what he told you, he was not the innocent party in our little disagreement three weeks ago. Nor was it a chance meeting. I found them harassing the daughter of one of your more well-known citizens. She fears to step forward and make the truth known, because of your habit of favoring the boy."

The magistrate sniffed. "A coquette, I'm sure. William would do no such thing."

"And thus you prove my point. I saw his behavior toward her. She is no more the coquette than the goodwife here."

The other man seemed to consider his words, then lunged for the table beside his bed. Sam was ready, had seen the twitch of the man's muscles, the shifting of his gaze. With a flick of his lash, he caught the leg of the bedside chest and yanked the piece of furniture across the floor. The magistrate fell with a crash, cursing, then scrambled to his feet.

"Get back in bed," Sam said, arm lifted for a second stroke. "My lady, do you stay put as well."

The goodwife sank back to her pillows, and the magistrate sat on the edge of the mattress, but made no other move to obey. "Look," he said, his voice holding the weariness of one not used to being challenged, "if you leave now, I promise to make it worth your while."

"You think I care about coin? Your son is a rogue and a scoundrel who preys on those weaker than him. This is not manhood. Neither is winking at his misbehavior, which you do. You bring shame on yourself and this town by continuing to pretend your son is innocent."

"You are one to speak," the magistrate said. "Appearing in a man's bedchamber at darkest night, terrifying him and his wife. If you want to be heard, petition the court."

"Your court isn't listening, lord magistrate. Your sense of justice is absent, and your son roves out of control. Any show of righteous indignation you might present me is a mockery of law."

"The mockery is you standing here, looking like a brigand."

"Like calls to like, perhaps. But be warned, your townspeople will not suffer this much longer. And if your son is brazen enough to do worse than he already has, I will see to it that he bears the consequences. Whether that is at my hand, or another's."

Without missing a beat, Sam flicked the lash out again, once more catching the table leg, and pulled it farther from the magistrate's reach. Then he stepped through the open window behind him and disappeared into the night.

The garden wall beckoned just below the balcony on which he perched. Behind him, the house erupted with the magistrate's bellow and the shriek of his wife. The hound set to baying again. Sam swung easily over the balcony rail and onto the edge of the garden wall, then ran the length of the wall to its far edge and over. He'd be well away before the magistrate roused anyone.

The thing now was returning to Jed before dawn, so they'd lose no time making the leg to Brewster's.

A day at Brewster's did indeed begin early. Too early. Not that Sally had slept a wink the night before.

The first vivid hues of sunrise rimmed the horizon when Sally decided that further lying abed was useless. She rose, washed and dressed with far more care than earlier, and made her way downstairs to kindle the hearth fires and begin preparations for another day of service at the inn.

A hum stirred in her throat as her hands flew, dividing bread dough and setting it in pans. The memory of the night's adventure brought a smile to her lips. It was more than the kisses—fervent enough to warm her cheeks even now—but, he'd said he'd return for her. Not soon, possibly. Part of their conversation had involved how folk spoke of his nickname, whether they thought him knave or hero, how he'd never intended either when he'd first begun, but now—

It might have been only a lark at first, she'd suggested, but perhaps God intended his role for something more. Perhaps this matter was larger than the two of them, although it had crossed her mind more than once that their meeting was not by chance.

She'd always believed in God, without question. Whether God truly took notice of her, now, was a different matter entirely. Why would the happiness of one simple innkeeper's daughter be of His concern?

But she'd been reared on Scripture, and Scripture said that not even a sparrow fell to the ground without His notice. Perhaps, then, He did care.

A rap on the back door startled her. Who could it be at this hour?

She stepped into the hallway to see—and the bulk outlined there made her blood run to ice.

Nay—oh nay—

"Papa!" she shouted, and fled toward the stairs.

"Sally Brewster, you will see me!" Willie's voice echoed through the hallway, and heavy footfalls thundered after. "You will hear me out, this moment!"

He caught up with her at the foot of the stairs, seized her shoulder, and flung her back against the wall. "Who are you to the Highwayman? Answer me!"

He punctuated his words with hard shoves. His breath, sour and stale, was hot on her face. She strained away, scrambling with fingernails and shoe to fend him off. He only leaned harder against her. "Tell me!"

She clenched her teeth against the words she longed to say. Curses did not become a woman.

"Listen to me, girl. You send that filthy brigand to my house, in the middle of the night, to wake my father and mother—you *will* suffer the consequences. It's more than a kiss I require of you, now."

"I'll never give myself to a serpent such as you," she gritted out.

"Giving does not enter into it any longer," he growled.

"And I'll make sure everyone in this town hears how you fled, whimpering, from the Highwayman's lash, after hiding behind me."

He flinched at that, then sneering, leaned in again—

"Unhand my daughter!"

Papa's snarl from the steps above them, and the business end of his musket, sent Willie reeling back. Sally let the wall continue to support her.

"Has your daughter told you how she has truck with rogues and brigands?" Willie said.

Papa was unflinching. "My daughter refuses to have truck with you. That is proof enough of her good taste." The musket barrel twitched. "Now move. If you darken the door of my establishment again, I'll shoot you on sight."

Willie straightened his clothes. "You'll rue this, I promise." His glare shifted to Sally. "Both of you."

She dared not breathe till he'd slunk back down the hall and out the door. Then all strength went out of her in a rush, and she slid to the floor.

"Sally, darling. Did he hurt you?"

Papa clattered down the remaining stairs, clad only in his shirt, grey hair loose to his shoulders, and set the musket against the wall before kneeling next to her.

"Nay—I—he—I'm well enough." But she couldn't seem to catch her breath.

Her thoughts still stuttered with the implications of Willie's words.

The Highwayman had paid a visit to the magistrate? On her behalf?

She wasn't sure whether to feel amazed, grateful, or betrayed.

Covering her face with both hands, she bent to her knees. *Oh God, if You do care—please help us!*

Chapter 9

Sam sat up, pushing aside bundles that had fallen on him with the jostling of the wagon bed. He scrubbed a hand across his face and peered at the deepening shadows. The sun had disappeared behind the stretch of mountains to their west. "Where are we?"

Jed laughed, but softly. "Still about a mile above Brewster's. Get any sleep?"

"Mm. Maybe."

Sam had found Jed pacing that morning, Brutus and Nero already yoked and restless to be on their way, when he'd pulled into the stableyard an hour past dawn. Jed eyed the lathered horse but said nothing for a change as Sam handed him the bundle of his costume, carefully wrapped in a wool blanket, and then paid the stableboy extra for the care of the hired horse. After explaining at least some of the night's events—all he was prepared to share with his cousin—he took Jed up on his offer to let him sleep it off while Jed drove.

"Well, you better look sharp for your ladylove, if you don't want her guessing who you are."

Sam finished rearranging the load then climbed back over the seat. "Tell me about it."

He ran his tongue across his teeth and winced at how fuzzy his mouth felt.

"And tomorrow is the Sabbath, aye? So we'll need to stay through." Jed elbowed him. "Not that you'll complain about that."

Sam made a noncommittal sound. Under other circumstances, nay. But when he considered how carefully he needed to guard himself now. . .

A deeper misgiving simmered inside him. Maybe it was naught but the wretched sleep he'd snatched throughout the day, but something niggled at the edges of his heart and mind. Something centered on Sally, more than the aching to see her.

And that was a fire he needed to bank, given that it might be a good long while before he'd have her in his arms again.

"We've not been to meeting in Staunton before, have we?" Jed said.

"Nay."

Up over the last hill—thankfully the ground was drier than last time—and the neat inn and stableyard of Brewster's, with the orchard stretching beyond, came into view in the twilight. On the opposite side of the road, the tendril of the river branch snaked its way through the valley.

Sam's throat tightened. Would he even be able to keep from speaking to Sally, from reaching for her?

What a difference from last time he'd faced her as himself.

Nero and Brutus broke into a trot, recognizing one of their usual havens. "Haw!" Jed shouted, as they neared the stableyard. The oxen obediently swung right, and Jed shouted for them to halt. Calls of greeting came from both the inn and barn.

Sally's twin brothers ran out from the barn to help with unyoking the oxen. "Jed!" Johnny piped. "What word of the Highwayman?"

Sam ignored the chill that swept him and kept to the task

of unfastening gear.

"Why, none that I know of, Johnny boy," Jed answered, just as he and Sam had agreed. "Right surprising, that."

"Huh. Well, Papa and Sally will be asking as well. Not sure why she's taken the sudden notice, but there's no figuring girls."

Jed laughed, and Sam ducked aside from his cousin's sharp glance.

"Willie Brown seems to think she knows something about him, though," Johnny went on, "which is why Papa's taken an interest. . ."

Just keep moving. Keep working.

Of course Willie Brown thought she'd know. She was there when the Highwayman had shamed him before his cronies. But had he seen them together last night, as well? It was possible, though he'd thought he'd been vigilant enough, and the orchard had yielded no sounds but those from his horse.

And their laughter, grown so loud a time or two that they'd had to shush themselves, which only led to more laughter.

"What are you grinning about, cousin? Get the other end of this yoke, will you?"

Sam swiped a hand down his face. Jed didn't need his help with the beam, but it was a good reminder to wake up.

A dozen or so other travelers were here, judging by the horses penned outside the barn and already in stalls. "Lucky to get lodging tonight, looks like," Jed commented.

Inside, Mr. Brewster met them and waved at an empty table. "Come in and welcome, but I'm afraid the rooms are all spoken for. It'll be the barn loft for you two, if you don't mind."

"Not at all," Jed said.

Sam scanned the great room as they seated themselves—no sign of Sally, but that was nothing to be wondered at. Mr. Brewster brought them both tankards. "You'll pardon us as well for being a bit slow," he said. "It's been something of a long day for all of us."

His gaze measured them both as they sampled the watered ale.

"Fine brew, as always," Sam offered.

Mr. Brewster nodded, but absently. "Thank you." A frown gathered between graying brows. "You wouldn't have heard aught of the Highwayman, would you?"

"Ah, no," Jed said easily. "Swallowed up by other news on this trip up the Great Road, seems like. Everyone's full of talk about the delegates meeting in Philadelphia for the continental congress—"

"Good, good." The frown deepened. "If you hear aught, would you kindly let me know?"

The man's manner was too distracted to escape Sam's notice, even with him watching for Sally. "Is there some trouble, sir?"

Mr. Brewster sighed, his gaze on the table. "I hesitate to share tales, but you are good lads. And praying men, if I recall."

Both Sam and Jed nodded, slowly.

"One of the last incidents surrounded the son of our chief justice. Apparently there was another last night, also involving my Sally, and the chief justice is threatening to have her arrested for slander."

Sam was half out of his chair before he realized it.

Mr. Brewster's sharp gaze twinkled. "I do not blame your outrage, son. But there's little you can do. Only—pray."

Sam sank back into his chair. "Aye, sir," he managed,

after a moment.

Oh, Sally. . .

The older man's gaze held his in something between a frown and a smile. "And I warn you, if you think well of my daughter at all, you'll find a way to soon speak your mind. Before another claims her affections."

~*~*~*~

In all, it had been a perfectly wretched day. Sally pushed the wisps of hair back from her face and shifted, one foot to another, but the aching there would not cease. The tenderness across shoulders and arms would be worse tomorrow, after she'd slept—and oh, how she needed to sleep.

Deepest was the dread and ache of her heart. It had been all day, with one task after another, in between visits from the sheriff and two of his deputies, and the chief justice himself, then a deluge of travelers that arrived just an hour ago.

The sheriff at least, at Papa's pleading, was unwilling to haul her immediately to the gaol. The magistrate fussed and foamed before Papa's calm insistence that aye, Willie had indeed accosted his daughter, in her own home, and he'd not stand for her being so accused.

Slander, indeed. And no one had seen hide nor hair of Willie, since. That was what chilled her most.

What are you to the Highwayman?

And then from Papa, gently, but much harder to resist, *Why would he ask you such a thing?*

She'd no idea if they'd been seen. They laughed a little too hard together at moments, likely talked too loudly as well. If Willie was looking for opportunity. . .

And so, still reeling from Willie's attack, to the shock of both Papa and Mama, she'd admitted the truth.

I am in love with the Highwayman, Papa. And he says he is with me. . .aye, I know I was foolish to go out with him to the orchard, but he behaved with honor, he did. . .

Her eyes burned every time she thought of it.

A step warned her that someone approached, and she looked up to see Papa. He'd lingered close today, but then, he hadn't let Mama far out of his sight either.

"The Wheeler boys are here," he said, very softly. "Tired and hungry, both of them, by the looks of it. Take them the usual."

Ah, not Sam. Not tonight.

"Aye, Papa." She reached for a tray, but stopped at his hand on her forearm. "Go gently with young Sam. They had no news of the Highwayman, but when I mentioned the day's trouble, Sam took it especially ill." He drew a deep breath. "I—I realize he may not be your first choice, sweet daughter, but do not rule him out. Just yet."

She swallowed past the fist-sized lump in her throat. "Aye."

'Twas stew again, midsummer fare full of squash and cabbage and other vegetables, with bread left over from morning. Her hands arranged the two meals as they always did, without thought, though her heart was leaden. With a deep breath, she lifted her aching shoulders and carried the tray out into the great room.

For a moment, the hum of voices overwhelmed her. There, against the opposite wall. And of course, the moment she'd come into view, Sam's head lifted, his gaze searching hers.

His expression remained still, but a telltale flush crept across his face. By the heat of her cheeks, hers matched in color, she was sure. She held herself steady, weaving through the tables and flashing the occasional apologetic smile to those she brushed past.

And his gaze remained on her, even when she reached the table and set the tray down. "Jed. Sam. Good evening to you both."

"Evening, Sally," Jed answered, reaching for his bowl.

With the ghost of a smile, Sam dipped a nod. "Thank you most kindly," he murmured.

She ventured a smile in return then hurried back to the kitchen.

There. She'd at least been civil. But tomorrow was the Sabbath, and as travel constituted breaking such, the boys would likely stay the extra day.

What would she do then?

Chapter 10

The two of them retired to the barn as soon as they'd finished supper. Jed brushed out Nero, while Sam tended Brutus.

He'd never seen Sally struggle so visibly to put on a brave face. What had happened to douse all that light and joy?

A pair of pert faces appeared above the stall door. "Hey Sam. Can we help?"

"Another forkful of hay would not be amiss."

The boys ran off, bickering over who would fetch it. "Both of you bring some," Jed called.

That settled it. Jacky took his armful to Jed, while Johnny brought his to Sam.

"So what was the big kerfuffle with Willie Brown and the sheriff today?" Sam asked.

"Oh, well, 'twas the strangest thing. Willie nearly broke down the door this morn at dawn. We heard him shouting at Sally, but Papa sent him packing at the end of his musket."

Redness seeped in at the edges of Sam's vision. Willie had been to the inn? And accosted Sally?

"Good for your papa," he said.

"Aye!" Johnny laughed, caught up in his tale. "Well, not two hours later, the justice and the sheriff came. The justice swears Sally is guilty of slander and demands the sheriff clap her in irons. Papa, however, said 'twas no slander when he'd witnessed Willie treating Sally roughly, in her own house."

Sam braced one hand on Brutus's broad back and stared across at Jed. His cousin looked every bit as stricken as he felt.

"What I want to know"—Johnny scratched his head—"is why all this talk of the Highwayman got mixed up in it. How could Sally know him?"

"Did you hear what Willie said to her this morning?" Sam asked.

"No, just he was shouting something about the Highwayman. Like he blames Sally for the trouble he's in now. Papa sent us upstairs when Sally said she needed to talk to him and Mama alone. We tried to listen, but they went to the other side of the house so we couldn't."

He gave a halfhearted grin, which Sam could not bring himself to answer.

"La, Sam. You ain't angry, are you?"

He unclenched his hand from the brush and forced a stiff smile. "Not at you, lad. Not at you."

This was his own fault, exposing her to retaliation from that cur.

He exchanged a long look with his cousin then turned back to the boys. "Thank you for your help. Run along back to your papa, before he has cause to worry."

They nodded, looking confused, but did as they were told. Sam waited until the door shut. "This happened because of me."

"Nonsense, Sam—"

"It did, and you know it." He turned, and with rare temper, slung the brush across the barn. Catching a little of his ire, Brutus sidestepped, and Sam shoved him back, then left the stall and latched it after himself. "I want to kill him, Jed. I won't, but—" He let out a hard breath. "If he thinks somehow that she's responsible for my visit to his father last night, he won't let it lie. I know the type, and so do you."

Jed nodded slowly.

Sam raked both hands through his hair and turned a circle, staring around the barn without seeing. "I can't leave her to this. I can't."

"I know."

He swung back toward his cousin. "You do?"

Jed gave a short laugh. "You have it so bad, Sam. But aye." He stepped closer. "We're here until day after tomorrow. We'll figure something out between now and then."

Sabbaths were naturally grave, austere days. Sally understood that. Yet she'd never endured one so unrelentingly awful.

First, of all the folk who lingered at the inn because of the Sabbath and attended meeting with them, 'twas Sam she had to end up sitting next to. As if there were an attachment between them, truly. And Papa and Mama encouraged it because, as they said, it might discourage Willie Brown if he thought Sam was courting her.

Sam was a strapping boy, to be sure, but. . .so very quiet.

And she could feel him watching her, all day, except possibly when they were sitting in meeting together. Even then she was aware of him in a way every bit as unnerving as when those blue eyes were actually on her.

After a simple lunch, some went back to meeting, but she and Papa stayed home to tend things that simply couldn't be left undone even on the Sabbath. But the quiet, and the waiting, pressed in on her, and she found herself walking out to the stableyard, where Sam was occupied at some task involving a wheel fitting on his wagon. His company was better than none, and at least she might be reasonably safe if Willie came to call again.

He looked up from beneath his flat-brimmed hat. His hands stilled for a moment before he nodded and went back to his work.

"What are you doing?" she asked, for lack of anything better to say.

He was quiet so long, she nearly gave up and returned to the house. "Axle's cracking. Just trying to reinforce it."

His voice sounded strange, pinched. Was it because of her? Did she somehow make him afraid to speak?

"You didn't have to stay this afternoon."

Another glance upward. "Your father said there'd been trouble."

"Aye." The admission was out before she could stop it. What was wrong with her lately? Maybe 'twas just that she'd known Sam for so long, he was comfortable to talk to.

She found a seat on a nearby barrel.

He'd stopped to watch her again. "Must you do that?" she said.

"Do what?"

"Look at me."

His head went down, his hands busied themselves again, but. . .was that a blush creeping up his neck, beneath the blond queue?

"You are very nice to look at," he said at last.

Sally felt her mouth fall open, and she could not breathe—could not speak. Her heartbeat was suddenly painful.

She snapped her eyes shut, then her mouth. *Oh, Highwayman! Where are you?*

Oh, Lord, help me.

It seemed to be all she could pray of late.

"Have I said aught to upset you?"

"I—nay—"

Sam straightened. "Is there someone who already claims your affections?"

Oh, she could not breathe—

"Aye. There is." She slid down from the barrel. "Forgive me."

Still gazing at her, he gave her a slow, sweet smile.

'Twas too much. Clutching her skirts in both hands, she fled for the house.

Chapter 11

The close of another fine day in the lower Valley. Orange and pink dusted the western mountains, above the inn and orchard. Sam chewed the end of a grass blade and could not rid himself of the sense of foreboding.

"I don't like it, by half," he said to Jed. "I expect Willie stayed hid for the Sabbath, but I wouldn't put it past him to try something tonight. Or tomorrow, once he knows another bunch of travelers have moved on."

Jed cracked open one eye from where he lay stretched in the grass, arms above his head. "I've been thinking, I could take the wagon, finish the run home. You could stay. . .except, how would you explain it to Mr. Brewster, let alone Sally, if you aren't willing to tell her yet?"

Sam shook his head. "I want to. I just. . .don't feel it's time yet."

She'd nearly rent his heart, the way she'd tried to be kind to him, as himself, but then avowed her affections to be with another—not knowing it was him.

Lord, forgive me for deceiving her.

'Twould be so easy to tell her. Unpack the coat, take it to her. . .*Sally love, I am the Highwayman.*

Too easy. And 'twould solve nothing, because he still had nothing to offer her.

"I could leave with you tomorrow morning," he went on, "hire a horse at the next ordinary, ride back. But. . ."

"But that would be leaving them alone for part of the day." Jed sat up, his expression grave.

"Precisely." Sam threw the stalk of grass away.

"Maybe it's time to let someone else in on the secret."

Sam stared at his cousin.

Jed laughed. "You want to really be in her father's good graces? Take him into your confidence. Mr. Brewster is a sensible man, and he'd be a good ally. And. . .I believe he would appreciate knowing he has one, as well."

Sam pulled a fresh grass stalk and chewed the end. This, now, seemed. . .right.

"Aye. Let's do that, then."

Mr. Brewster lifted a brow to their request to speak with him, but made no comment as he followed them outside the inn and to the barn. Gut churning, Sam likewise said nothing but went straight to the wagon, pulled the small chest from under the seat, and turned to the older man. "Where might we have privacy, sir?"

Mr. Brewster considered the chest, then Jed, then Sam. "Follow me."

He led them to a storage shed at the rear of the inn. Inside, Sam set down the chest, crouched beside it, and laid both hands flat across the top. He blew out a breath, but it didn't ease the iron band around his chest. "So you'll know," he said to Mr. Brewster, "that I do not willingly play false with anyone."

Slowly, he swung open the lid then lifted out the hat and set it aside. The black silk handkerchief came next, then the coat, its buttons and embroidery glinting in the dying light. Lastly were the boots. Draping the black silk over his shoulder, Sam rose and faced Mr. Brewster, the coat in one hand, the boots in the other.

The older man gazed at the ensemble for a long moment, folded his arms, and rubbed one hand across his mouth before a grin broke across his features. "Well. Great glory above. You are the Highwayman."

He began to chuckle, and the tightness around Sam's chest loosened. He and Jed exchanged a wild grin.

"It is Sam, and not you, aye?" the older man asked, turning to Jed.

Jed laughed. "Aye. All him."

"Not quite, you rascal," Sam said. "You egged me on."

"What of the whip?" Mr. Brewster asked.

Sam returned boots and coat to the chest before reaching down inside his shirt for the coiled whip. "I've been carrying it since last night."

Mr. Brewster's eyes gleamed. He glanced again at Jed. "Is he as good with that thing as they say?"

"Better," Jed said, straightening.

"Well, well. Won't Sally have the shock of her life?" He sobered, fastening Sam with a stern look. "What is your intention where she's concerned?"

"To somehow prove worthy of her, sir."

A fine, misting rain blew across the mountains overnight, and Sally woke with a dull ache lingering in her breast. The inn's morning routine was oddly comforting as she poured griddle cakes and cooked sausages for the travelers before they ventured out into the wet.

Though foolish of her to expect it, she'd risen during the night to sit at her window, listening and waiting in case the Highwayman came. Surely, if he cared, he'd hear of Willie Brown's visit and call on her again. Unless he was already too far away.

Regardless, she'd not sit up night after night for him. No matter how sweet his kisses and his laughter, or how pretty his compliments. She'd work to do, after all, and if he intended to return, it would not be any sooner for her pining.

Her eyes burned, and she rubbed her forearm across them.

As she turned from the fire, a movement at the kitchen door caught her eye. It was Sam. Watching her, of course. "Aye?" she choked.

"Jed and I be leaving. Just wanted to offer our thanks and bid you good day."

Again, that strange pinch to his voice. Although he cut a neater figure than customary, with high boots tied over the knee—were those his usual ones?—and a black cloth around his neck, beneath the checked linen shirt and plain brown waistcoat.

Fine dress, for a drover headed out into the rain.

"And to you," she managed.

With a nod, he turned and disappeared from sight.

She went back to work, but her throat ached. She'd been so unkind to him yesterday. She should at least offer an apology—

When she dashed to the hallway, he was gone.

~*~*~*~

Three days of waiting and watching, through drizzle and wind and hot sun. Sam had a beautiful view of the inn and orchard, not to mention spectacular sunrises and sunsets, but 'twas enough to stretch anyone's patience. He could have made the drive home to Charlotte Town and back before Willie would show again. . .but then, he'd no way of knowing that, for sure.

A tramping through the laurels alerted him to someone's

approach. Likely Mr. Brewster, bringing him dinner.

An ally indeed, the man had been. Faithfully fetching him food or other needed items, making the walk himself since he didn't trust the boys not to talk. And Sally—it pained Sam to keep her uninformed, but because she'd asked to not know, they'd judged it best to keep the Highwayman's secret at least until after Willie was found.

Sam rose to greet the man he hoped to gain as a father-in-law when all this was over. "Has Sally noticed the missing provisions yet?"

"Not yet." He grinned and handed Sam a covered pail. "Fresh stew and biscuits."

Sam hummed his appreciation and wasted no time sitting down and digging in. "Any word?" he asked, between bites.

Mr. Brewster frowned, gazing out over his land. "Rumor has it, Willie was seen lurking about his home but vanished again. He can't show up quickly enough, in my opinion. Sally still flinches at every small sound."

"Hmm." Sam waved the spoon. "If there's nothing tonight, I'll go roving farther out."

The older man nodded shortly then gave him a slight smile. "My thanks. For staying, for being willing to see this out." A sharper look this time. "And for behaving yourself while being so close to my daughter. I'm astonished at how easily led astray she is by you."

Sam ducked his head. 'Twasn't entirely by choice that he hadn't lured Sally back out to the orchard these past several days. The temptation became especially strong a time or two when he'd glimpsed her at her attic window. "I am determined to see this matter through." He chewed and swallowed. "To—have something to offer her when this is finished."

Mr. Brewster tipped his head. "I think you have more already than you know."

"I'm honored you think so, sir."

'Twould seem cold comfort later, he was sure, when the night closed in and he found himself drifting like a ghost around the orchard and inn yard, but for now, the man's confidence warmed him.

Mr. Brewster left just before sunset, and once dark had fallen, Sam also made his way down the mountainside. Time to begin his customary night patrol.

He'd kept the boots and handkerchief with him, tied the tops in place like cavalry boots. A sliver of disappointment still cut him that Sally hadn't noticed. . .but then, details of his boots had likely been lost in the shadows when they'd met, and one black handkerchief could look like another.

The coat and hat, however, he'd left in the storage shed. It was easier just to slip inside and—

Tonight, the door of the shed stood ajar. Sam withdrew into shadow and looked around, but there was no sound.

Inside the shed, the chest stood empty.

Chapter 12

Sally made a last walk through the great room, wiping down tables and straightening chairs. Her feet ached, but not as badly as a few nights ago, and she'd managed to sleep decently despite rising every few hours to peer out her window.

She sighed. Tonight she wouldn't sit up for him. Truly.

All was tidied and ready for tomorrow. Above, she could hear her parents moving about their chamber, and the more distant thump of the boys roughhousing while they were supposed to be settling to bed. As if on cue, Mama's voice called out to them.

Sally chuckled. Ah, she could almost believe life was returning to the usual—

A heavy pounding came on the great room door. She froze then reached for a lamp, but backed toward the hallway and stairs. She would not, under any circumstances, go answer the door alone.

The pounding came again, more insistently.

"Papa?"

His swift footsteps answered, across the floor and down the steps.

Thud! Thud! Thud! Whoever was there had resorted to a concerted effort to break the door in. With a splintering crash, it swung inward.

"Papa-a-a!"

Sally could not suppress the scream tearing itself from her throat—and then she could not breathe at all.

The man filling the doorway wore the hat and coat she'd come to love—but the face bore the hated grin of Willie Brown.

No! No no no no. . .

Papa was there beside her, musket raised. "Get out of my inn!"

Four others crowded in behind Willie, all masked, all bearing pistols and muskets. Willie held a pistol, too, she now noticed. The men fanned out, surrounding Sally and her father.

"An hour with Tall Sally. That's all I want, and no one will be hurt," Willie said.

"You evil rascal," Papa growled. "You'll not touch my daughter."

"Of course I will." Willie stepped forward and reached toward her, but she slapped his hand away. "Come now, don't make this any more difficult." He lifted his arms, turning them so the buttons and braid glimmered in the lamplight. "What do you think of my new coat, Sally?"

As a knife in her breast, was what she thought. She dragged in a breath through the cutting pain. "You aren't worthy even to touch it."

Willie laughed. "But it's the coat of your lover, sweet Sally. Could I not be him?"

"Not now, nor ever."

"And where is he?"

As Willie glanced about, Sally forced herself to calm, and to look closely at the coat. It was even more fabulously embroidered than she'd seen by moonlight. But more importantly—no blood, no rips. No sign of wear since the last time she'd spent time in the company of its owner. That possibly meant no violence done him. Perhaps Willie had merely found it, and the Highwayman himself was alive and well.

"He will be here," she said. "He will come for you."

Willie looked into her eyes with another terrible smile. "I am counting on just that."

He nodded to the others and lunged toward her. An awful scuffle ensued—someone knocked into Papa, his musket went off, then one of the pistols.

Sally threw herself out of Willie's reach, toward the hearth. If she could but get to one of the pokers—

Willie's arm closed about her neck, and she fought for release. The lamp fell from her fingers. A crash, and fire bloomed in front of her.

With a curse, Willie hauled her back, but the edge of her petticoat and apron were on fire. "Let me go!" she cried.

Miraculously, she was free, and with shaking hands she unpinned and untied apron and outer petticoat and kicked them away. The rest of her skirts were not yet ablaze, and she was seized again.

"Nay!" she shrieked, as Willie dragged her outside. "Papa!"

Arms like bands of iron held her fast. "Mama!" she screamed. "Fire! Everyone out!"

With ragged breaths, she could only watch as in ones and twos, his cronies fled the spreading fire, and upstairs, shouts turned to cries.

Please, Lord! Please oh please, let them escape safely! Whatever happens to me, let them be safe.

The fire spread unbelievably fast. "Oh God, please!" she moaned, then collapsed, sobbing, against Willie's arms. "Save them, please. I'll do anything! Only get my family out alive."

But with an ugly laugh, he pulled her away, deeper into the shadows.

She let loose with the only thing she had left—a long, high, tearing cry that echoed across the valley.

It couldn't have been the boys who found the chest, they'd have made immediate outcry. Sam searched everywhere—the barn and its loft, the cattle pens, the whole of the orchard—but found no trace of an intruder. He was on the hillside above the orchard, half a mile from the inn, when he heard the distant pounding.

That was not a late traveler seeking lodging for the night.

The coiled whip already in his hand, Sam fairly flew down the hill, through the orchard. Flames danced behind the windows of the great room by the time he rounded the barn.

Lord, have mercy! It had become his favored prayer of late.

Several figures crowded around the front—were they the Brewster family and guests, or—? He could not pick out smaller figures of women and children.

Then came a wild scream that raised every hair on his neck and arms, issuing from just down the hill from the inn.

Oh, God. Sally.

And those men were doubtless Willie Brown's gang.

He had to choose—those still inside, or Sally? The hostler and other stable hands were spilling from their lodgings now, and he waved toward the inn. "Make sure everyone gets out! I'll deal with the miscreants."

~*~*~*~

"Where is your lover now?" Willie hissed in Sally's ear as he hauled her, kicking and snarling, down the hill.

"He'll come! Never doubt that."

He stopped in the lee of a rocky outcropping, just above the road, and fetched her about. From below came the stamps and snorts of several horses.

She met the gleam of his eyes with all the defiance she could muster. "Murder as well as ravishing now, aye? What did you promise those boys, that they'd follow you to such depths?"

A deep growl issued from his chest, but before he could speak, a report echoed from the hill above them. And then another, followed by a cry.

Willie cursed. "I told them not to shoot unless necessary—"

But Sally felt a laugh bubbling inside her. "That's no shot. It's a whip crack."

Sure enough, the voice she'd come to love called out, "Rogues and scoundrels! Did you not learn your lesson the first time?"

Sally wrenched out of Willie's grasp and scrambled up the hill. With another curse, he caught her and pinned her to the ground.

More cracks, followed by howls and pleas for mercy. The fire illuminated well down the hill now, where men were running from the town, coming to their aid.

Sally kicked against Willie's hold. She realized, dimly, that he was without the coat. Where had he left it? "There's no place for you to hide, Willie Brown! He's found you."

Please, Lord, let him hurry!

"He'll have to come pry you from my fingers himself—"

"'Twould be my pleasure, blackguard."

Sally caught only a glimpse of a dark form outlined against the fire before Willie shoved her away and fumbled for his pistols. A shot went off at the same time as the whip crack, but it was Willie who cried out, hoarsely.

The shadowy figure drove him back. "You—will never—touch this woman—again," he said, each phrase accompanied by the lash.

She couldn't help it—he was so terrible, so like an avenging angel, she had to bury her face in her arms.

And then Willie was gone, having run away sobbing into the dark like a small boy.

A pair of hands took her gently by the shoulders. "Sally—Sally love—"

It was him, it truly was. She pushed off the ground, let him help her rise and turn her around—

And there, in the light from the burning inn, she thought she recognized Sam.

A sob clogged her throat, then another. She covered her mouth with both hands to silence herself.

"Sally," he sighed. "Are you hurt?"

The voice was right—and the whip—aye, he still held it in his hand. But he stood still, watching her, waiting. His chest rose and fell with breaths that matched her own.

"Sam?" 'Twas naught but a squeak.

Another sigh. "Aye. 'Tis me, Sally."

"It was you—all the time?"

"It was."

She fought back another sob or three.

He held out a hand. "Come. Let's get you back to your family."

"They are safe?"

A half smile lifted his mouth. "Aye."

Oh, thank You, Lord! Still she could not move. Her

thoughts spun back over the past days—the past weeks. The looks and the smiles and the funny way he'd had of saying his words of late.

And she thought of when the Highwayman came to her rescue in the orchard, what sounded like shock in his voice, and—

The kisses. All those kisses. The way he'd held her, as if—as if he truly did love her.

Sam Wheeler was the Highwayman. She'd kissed quiet Sam Wheeler.

His hand was still outstretched. Without another word, she took it and let him lead her up the hill, to where the inn burned high, but Papa sat on the grass with Mama's arms around him, and the boys huddled close. She ran to them.

Papa didn't let her hold onto him long, but pushed her away. "Go on, girl, he's waiting for you."

She stood and looked where he nodded. Aye, it was still Sam, whip yet unfurled, his face etched with what looked like pain.

"You knew?" she said, to Papa.

"Aye. He confided in me late on the Sabbath. He felt responsible for Willie's last attack and wanted to make sure we were kept safe."

"At which task I failed miserably," Sam said.

"You couldn't have known," Papa said.

"I came down this evening to find the coat and hat missing."

"Aye." To Sally's surprise, Papa chuckled. "Your girl here, she never doubted you for a moment."

"Where's the coat now?" she asked.

"I think it caught fire when you dropped that lamp," Papa said.

She looked at the fire, and to her dismay, her eyes filled.

"All your hard work, Papa."

"We'll get it back, sweet girl."

Slowly, she turned to Sam. He looked entirely different—harder, sure of himself.

"If you'd be willing, sir," he said, "I'd be pleased to stay and help you rebuild."

"Help would be welcomed. And what of after?"

Sam shifted and met Sally's gaze. "That, sir, depends upon your daughter."

Chapter 13

He'd never seen her more beautiful—cap gone, hair loosed about her shoulders, dirt smudging her face.

Tears in her eyes as she stared at him, openmouthed. Like she still couldn't believe it.

Well, he'd a lot of years of silence to make up for.

Her eyes narrowed, her lips firming for a moment. "Did you mean anything you said to me? Out there in the orchard?"

"I meant all of it." He stepped toward her. "Every word, Sally. I have loved you since—oh, I can't remember when. But not until the night you first met me as the Highwayman could I bring myself to speak."

She swallowed, and her lips parted again. "That was a lot of words for Samuel Wheeler. . .but spoken like the Highwayman." She closed some of the distance between them. "Courtly. Gallant, even."

He felt a smile tugging at his mouth. "Jed and his family always did say I was too bookish, by half."

She stepped nearer, skimmed his chin and jaw with her fingertips. A slight frown warred across her features, and she sniffed. "The Highwayman was too bold, by half, for a girl he'd never courted before."

"Aye, that he was." His hand stole out to touch the waves of hair falling across her shoulders, shimmering like the fire it reflected. "He might be forgiven, perhaps, if it were known that he intended to reveal all and make it right."

She gulped a breath, sniffled—and suddenly was in his arms. He gathered her close, breathing her in.

"Aye. Oh, aye. This is familiar." She shook in his embrace—was that a laugh? She tipped back her head, one hand still on his face, the other at the back of his neck, and gave another watery chuckle. "I'd never imagined the Highwayman with fair hair and blue eyes." She met his gaze. "Nor that it was Sam Wheeler I'd kissed."

"And what of now? Can you bear the thought of kissing him again?"

"I don't know, let me see." And there in front of her family and half the town, she pulled him in.

Lost in her sweetness, he was dimly aware of the cheer that rose around them.

When she drew away, eyes shining, she said, "I can bear it, I think. But only if you promise to kiss me like that every day for the rest of my life."

His grin stretched from ear to ear, and the blaze in his cheeks surely matched that of the inn, beside them. "I will most certainly do my best, sweet lady mine."

~*~*~*~

They'd stood hand in hand when the magistrate arrived, fuming and sputtering at the sight of his son in irons. The other four young men had been likewise arrested. The sheriff, so easily swayed before, now shook his head to the magistrate's demands. The men of the town had enough of Willie Brown's misbehavior, and the burning of Brewster's inn provided the final straw for them.

The sheriff was still an elected official, they reminded him, and liked his job. And if the chief justice wanted to keep his, he'd stop subverting justice. The tide of change had begun, and they'd no longer stand for anything smacking of tyranny.

Papa and Sam had a quiet talk with the sheriff after. Because none but Willie had been seen wearing the Highwayman's coat, and none could say with any surety who the original owner was—and said coat had disappeared somewhere in the inferno that was the inn—the sheriff saw no reason to do aught but drop the matter. Let the Highwayman disappear as all legends did, into the mists of time.

Sally felt a touch of sadness at the loss of that beautiful coat. But truth be told, 'twas the man inside she loved—not the costume.

And Sam still sported those tall boots. Sally smiled as she realized why they'd seemed so familiar that one morning.

He turned, as if he knew she watched him, and met her gaze across the stableyard. His eyes widened, and then he gave her that unbearably sweet smile which had so broken her heart on Sabbath's evening.

Sam—her Sam—the Highwayman.

Who would have thought it?

Author's Note

Thank you for reading this slightly updated version of *The Highwayman!* You may notice elements from several other stories from across the years, ranging from the Alfred Noyes epic poem of the same title (with a happier ending), to Zorro (of course) and Indiana Jones—and not least of all, one of my favorite scenes from Laura Ingalls Wilder's *Farmer Boy,* where the quiet, mild-mannered teacher takes on the school bullyboys with a bullwhip, borrowed from Almanzo Wilder's father.

Defending Truth

The text of this story previously appeared in *A Pioneer Christmas Collection* by Barbour Publishing. It has since been modified and updated.

For all of you who believed, even when I dared not.

Acknowledgements

(new to the 2022 edition)

This story represents thirty years of waiting on my very first publishing contract. As such, I am indebted to so many who have helped and encouraged me on the journey. First and foremost was my mother, who passed away right after New Year's in 2016, who lived long enough for me to put the volume of *Pioneer Christmas* in her hands but had already lost so much of her eyesight that she couldn't read it for herself … so I read it to her. To her I owe countless chores done and defenses offered to my dad as I shut myself away in my room to write, oblivious to the outside world and sometimes especially to family obligations.

Then there was the small but dedicated group of my mother's friends, the readers (and fellow writers) to whom she bragged about my work when I was a mere teenager. Beckie, Michael, and Deb, I've never forgotten your kindness.

And the classmates who read my early work and enthused over it. Especially Kelly, who always handed back what I'd let her read and said, "It's good," even when it wasn't.

My friends in college, some of whom still remember (thank you, Kathy!), were also encouraging. Corey, who honored me with being impressed at the very thick typed manuscript I showed him. Leisha, who taught me much about the writing industry and mentored me in crafting query letters.

And, of course, my husband Troy—fellow

bibliophile, who was not only unbelievably supportive but introduced me (despite much protest) to the wonders of computer use and word processing.

All that was just within the first ten years of starting my first novel. Later—much later—the Lord sent me to a writing workshop for homeschoolers, where I met the peerless Christian western author Stephen Bly. God used him and his wife to set my feet back on the path to pursuing publication and encourage me to attend my first-ever writers conference.

In the meantime, I discovered that my good and dear friend Lee S. King, from an online community of homeschooling mothers-of-many, was also a writer. She's the one who helped me reclaim my book chapters from the wasteland of WordPerfect formatting.

I joined online writers groups and collected more friends and critique partners along the way. I had the thrill of meeting published authors—and discovering they, too, were very human and struggled as much at times with their stories as I did.

Every step of the way, Troy was there. Never complaining about the expense of writers conferences, never flagging in his enthusiasm for my stories, never doubting (at least that I heard) that someday I'd see my work in print.

And then one day—God popped open the door for this story to be born. I'm indebted both to my very good friend Elizabeth Goddard for nudging me to answer the call for submissions, and to our editor

Becky Germany of Barbour for taking the chance on a nobody writer. To other writing friends and mentors along the way—too many to list here. In particular, though, there was Susan May Warren, whose teaching finally helped me get a grasp on character goals and motivations (and communicate that to the page); Brandilyn Collins, whose articles on writing action and suspense helped me learn to amp the tension in my own writing—and who was kind enough at a conference to read a bit of an early story and give me baldly honest feedback; and Donita K. Paul, the dearest mentor and fantasy author ever. And those I walked beside as God opened the door to publication for them: Michelle Griep, Ronie Kendig, Jennifer Uhlarik.

A hearty continued thanks to my husband—and to the children God has given us. I may or may not have loosely modeled Truth's younger siblings after my youngest four.

And of course—to the Lord Himself, the Author and Finisher of our faith and ultimate witness to all the drama we humans create. As Francesca Battistelli sings, "It's all His stage—He knows my name!" That was the truth I had to grasp firmly before moving ahead on this journey.

Lastly, I am indebted to YOU, the reader, whose reviews and general encouragement have blessed me over and over again. Thank you for letting my stories be part of your journey as well!

Chapter One

Late October 1780

Papa would tan her hide if he knew she was out here, again. Too many Indians to worry about. Not to mention Tories, or British. But Papa was still gone, fighting the British, and the young'uns needed fed.

Truth Bledsoe took a better grip on her grandfather's long rifle and peered through the cold fog of the western North Carolina morning. The narrow path up the mountain lay beneath a carpet of reds and golds, slick with rain, all but a few yards ahead faded into the mist. The forest was still, except for the occasional drip and creak of branch.

With a deep breath, she trudged on, until out of the mist loomed a great boulder, tucked into a fold of the mountainside.

Her favorite hunting perch. She slid the rifle up over the edge, then with fingers and toes in various cracks, hoisted herself onto the top. There she settled herself to wait for whatever game might wander past.

She'd taken her share of deer, turkey, and squirrel from this rock. Seen the occasional panther. Even glimpsed a few Indians. Today, she was just hoping for something to fill the stew pot.

Her ears strained for shreds of sound. Everything

would be muffled in the fog, whether the whoosh of a deer's snort or the rustle of a squirrel in the leaves.

The snap of a twig, when it came, drew her almost straight up, gun to her shoulder.

"Don't shoot!" came a sharp cry.

Sighted there at the end of her rifle was a man—young, unkempt, hollow cheeked. Not one she recognized from the near settlements.

"Please. For the love of God, don't shoot."

She did not move or lower the rifle. She'd take no chances. "Who are you?"

"I—" He swallowed, dark gaze flicking over her.

No hat, no rifle, no gear to speak of, even a haversack. Filthy from head to toe. Tattered hunting frock and breeches, and were those—bloodstains?

"Answer," she said. "Now."

His already-pale face went a shade more grey. His mouth flattened, and his brows came down. "No one of consequence."

"So, there's no one to miss you if I shoot."

"I didn't say that!"

A wry smile tugged at the corner of her mouth. "Tell me, then, why I should not shoot you. Besides the love of God, of course."

Not a small reason, that.

He swayed a little on his feet. "Because ..." His voice dropped. "Because the battle is over."

Her heart hitched. The love of God, indeed.

She kept the rifle aimed—a girl must be prudent, after all—but lifted her head. Those were most certainly bloodstains, then. "Are you wounded?"

He shook his head.

"How long since you last ate?"

Behind the curtain of stringy brown hair, his dark eyes remained wary. One shoulder lifted, then fell.

Nothing for it, then. Venting a sigh, she propped the rifle against her hip, keeping it leveled toward him, and reached her other hand into her haversack. The man's gaze shifted, curious, hungry.

When she found the napkin-wrapped chunk of johnnycake, big as two of her fists, she pulled it out and tossed it to him. He caught it midair with only the slightest fumble.

"There," she said. "Eat up."

He didn't need to be told twice.

"Slowly. You'll choke, otherwise." She reached this time for her canteen, and swung it toward him. He easily snagged the strap as it sailed through the air.

Still eyeing her with caution and expectation, he unstoppered the wooden vessel and took a drink before making short work of the last handful of her flat cornbread.

"Nearly out of sugar, so 'tain't as sweet as I'd like," she said.

He wiped one sleeve across his mouth. "Tastes mighty fine. My thanks to you."

The rifle was getting heavy, but she ignored the burn in her arms and shoulders. "What battle, now?"

He stilled. His gaze darted to hers and away. "Kings Mountain."

The chill those words gave her went all the way from toes to scalp. *Lord, have mercy! He must be a Tory.*

~*~*~*~

He'd thought nothing could ever unsettle him again, not after the battle and the horrors he'd witnessed in the days following. Not even being held at gunpoint by a fierce over-the-mountain girl.

He'd thought wrong.

After the initial scare they'd given each other, Micah Elliot tried to keep his movements slow and steady. No telling how twitchy she might get with that rifle—and a fine one it was, too, a Pennsylvania model, as long as she was tall. The girl, now, he couldn't tell, wrapped as she was in a man's hunting frock, her head covered in a felt hat, one edge cocked and decorated with a turkey feather. Eyes as pale as the mist, and almost as cold, peered at him from beneath the brim, and her mouth was a thin line above a pointed chin.

He hadn't reckoned on her taking pity on him and giving him food, either, but he was right grateful for that. And he wasn't lying about the corncake being tasty.

"Now." Her eyes narrowed. "I know you're not from around here. Who are you and why are you here?"

How much could he trust her? Cols. Shelby and Sevier had at least tried to be fair after the battle, but he'd had a taste of the legendary savagery of the over-the-mountain men. Worse than Indians, it was said. Whether that was so, he could not say, but his body still carried the aches and bruises of their smoldering fury.

And his head was still a little swimmy, making it hard to pull his tattered thoughts together and come up with a defense. "Who are you, and why are *you* here?"

She hefted the rifle, and her faded blue skirt swayed a little, beneath the coat. "I asked first."

He fished, and came up with a short form of his middle name. "Will." That was common enough.

"Will ...?"

"Williams."

Did he imagine it, or did the corner of her mouth lift? Her gaze lost none of its fire. "Well, then, Will Williams. And from where do you hail?"

"East." The word was out before he could stop it.

"Oh, so amusing, you are." She tilted her head, and the misty light outlined a strong cheekbone and jaw. "Get a little johnnycake down your gullet, and you have all kinds of sass."

He wasn't going to tell her that the bread barely eased the ache in his gut. "Well, you did feed me. You're less likely to spend a rifle ball on someone you've just given your own provisions to."

But he stepped back a couple of paces, just to show his good will. No sense in tempting the pretty hand of Fortune.

"King's Mountain, you say." Her face resumed its grimness. "We heard tell of Ferguson's men meeting a bloody end there. You were on the Tory side, then?"

Right smart she was. He held his tongue. Nothing to say there.

"Well," she muttered. "At least you didn't lie about that."

"The truth means much to you?"

She gave him what approached a real smile. "My *name* is Truth. Truth Bledsoe. My uncle is captain of the home guard for our settlements."

Would it help his case or hurt it to tell her he was a coward? An escaped loyalist prisoner, who could no longer face how neighbor fought neighbor and brother fought brother, back home?

"Then I expect you're mighty handy with that rifle."

Her chin came up. "I'm near to fair."

Likely a crack shot, the way she handled it. He didn't want to test that.

"You going to tell me why you're here?" she asked, her voice low.

She stood, balanced in a small hollow in the side of the boulder, skirts swaying just a little, but she held that long rifle as steady as could be.

She had to be as scared of him as he was of her, maybe more.

"How long's it been since you ate?" she pressed.

"A week, maybe longer." And not much, even then. They weren't exactly generous with rations for prisoners.

Her mouth thinned a little more.

His gut growled, the hunger sharper than ever. It was becoming more difficult to keep the tremors out of his limbs, standing here under her eye. Better to take the chance of trusting her and die here, quickly, than of slow starvation. "I was part of the North Carolina militia, from above Charlotte Town. Those of us what didn't die at King's Mountain were taken by the rebels—I—I mean—"

She nodded slowly. "See? I knew you were Tory."

"Loyalist."

Her fingers lifted on the gun barrel. "Makes no never mind. Go ahead."

His heart pounded inside his chest so hard, he was sure she heard it. "They carried us to Gilbert Town. Nine of us were hanged. And the rest—"

He couldn't say the words. Couldn't inflict the horror of it on her, a mere girl—

But she'd fed him. She deserved an explanation.

"There was unspeakable abuse," he said. "You don't know," and he shook his head again.

"Ferguson threatened our settlements with unspeakable things," she said.

He swallowed. "I know what you must think of me, but I promise I mean you no harm. You, or the settlements. Regardless of what Ferguson said."

And how could he? He didn't even know where his loyalties lay anymore.

Chapter Two

What was I thinking?

Truth huffed. She'd stomp back down the trail if she weren't so particular about stepping downhill on wet leaves. She'd not just spared a Tory—one who'd doubtless faced her father across a battlefield—but fed him. And then bid him go back into hiding.

And she still didn't have anything to fill the pot, at home.

Telling him, *Shoo, go away, I need to finish hunting,* didn't sit well with her, but what could she do? He was noisy enough to scare away game for a mile in any direction. And he should know better.

She thought of the way he'd swayed, stumbled a little and caught himself. Bone weary, he'd looked ... maybe soul weary as well. And that was the reason she'd had pity on him and not only warned him back into hiding, but promised to bring him more food.

What *was* she thinking?

His plea still wrung at her. *For the love of God.* Likely he'd meant it as a common oath. Maybe. But maybe not.

Now, after wasting so much time, she had to see to her sisters and younger brother. Get off the mountain, back to the cabin, and while she was at it, see if Uncle Anthony had any word on Papa. It had been a good two weeks. If he was helping guard prisoners from the battle, then it could be a bit longer, and she'd learned not to fret overmuch when he was out riding with Col. Sevier and the others.

There was unspeakable abuse ... you don't know.

A chill swept her as the young man's words came back to mind. From Papa? Never. Oh, he could be stern. Specially after losing Mama three years back, there were times Truth wasn't sure he was still the Papa she'd always known. But maybe that was just on account of growing older, herself, and seeing life a bit more clearly.

But abuse? No. Maybe he'd lost his temper a time or two, but he was more likely to leave the cabin than take it out on her or the young'uns.

So, if Papa was there, that meant he either couldn't stop it, or—

She rounded a bend of the trail and skidded to a halt. There, outlined in the thinning mist, was a perfect six-point buck.

Ah Lord! Could it be? And in the unlikeliest of places, as well.

Without another thought, she swung the rifle to her shoulder, took aim, and squeezed the trigger. There was no turning down provision when it appeared for the taking.

The familiar recoil of the weapon slammed into her shoulder. Smoke puffed into the air and was lost in the fog. She peered again into the gloom—and there lay the buck, dropped with the single shot.

That surely was a miracle.

By long habit, she first reloaded the rifle. Afterward she made quick work of field dressing the animal, saving the organ meats, and tying the cord she always kept in her haversack to the buck's hind legs for dragging the carcass home. Now her main concern was leaving before a hungry bear caught wind of her kill.

Back at the cabin, her next youngest sister Patience had milked the cow and set the milk to rise, and Thomas had brought in wood. A bright, cheery fire warmed the inside of the cabin, and her two youngest sisters, Thankful and Mercy, were at their morning chore of brushing and braiding each other's hair.

Thomas's head came up at her entrance. "Fresh meat?"

Setting her rifle in the corner, she flashed him a grin. "A deer. Six-point buck."

His blue eyes rounded. With a whoop, he went to gather the knives and bowls they used for cutting up the meat.

She tugged off her hat, hung it on its peg. And how would she get food to—what was his name, Will?—without a dozen questions from the young'uns?

Will ... Williams. With a snort, she slid out of the worn, fringed hunting frock and hung it up as well.

Together, she knew they'd make short work of it—skinning, cutting the meat into strips for smoking, and saving aside a haunch for roasting. And little Mercy she set to the side on a chair, with the Bible open before her.

"Behold," Mercy read, her clear, high voice steady, "the heaven and the heaven of heavens is the Lord's thy God, the earth also, with all that therein is."

Truth thought of the wildness of the mountains. How great God must be, for shaping them.

"...For the Lord your God is God of gods, and Lord of lords, a great God, a mighty, and a terrible, which regardeth not persons, nor taketh reward: He doth execute the judgment of the fatherless and widow, and loveth the stranger, in giving him food and raiment. Love ye therefore the stranger: for ye were strangers in the land of Egypt."

Her hands slowed at her task. *Giving him food and raiment.* Well, that settled it. She had to do something about that half-starved, soon-to-be-naked man up the mountain, whether or not she liked it. She'd just have to figure out a way to do so without the others finding out.

Or Papa, once he returned.

There was only the pop and thunder of rifle and musket fire, the tang of smoke, the screams of the wounded, and those chilling war whoops from the rebel forces surrounding the mountain. Micah crouched, gripping the musket, his bayonet at the ready. Why was the colonel taking so long on the order to charge?

And over everything, Ferguson's whistle, with which he signaled above the din of battle. Would Micah even be able to hear the under-officer's order? He strained for the shout, but only the rebel screams and shriek of the whistle ripped at his eardrums. Still, none of his company moved yet, even when the fire pouring from below tore bloody holes in their hunting coats.

Inexplicably, Ferguson's whistle now sounded like a whippoorwill, each three-beat call punctuated by a rifle wound opening the breast of the man on Micah's right ...

He wrested himself awake with a gasp. Oh Lord, would he never stop dreaming about it?

As his eyes adjusted to the faint daylight outside the cave where he'd sheltered the last few nights, he heard again the call: *whippoorwill! whippoorwill!*

But it was deep autumn, long past the season the woodland bird would customarily take up the mournful, rhythmic melody that gave it its name. And the time of day was all wrong.

He sat up, crept to the mouth of the cave, and listened. Silence, then more slowly, *Whip...poor...will?*

Heart pounding, he put two fingers to his lips, then hesitated. Indians sometimes used such calls, but something inside told him it wasn't an Indian. That over-the-mountain girl—*Truth*—aye, a severe name for an equally severe female—had promised to bring him more food.

Not for the first time, he cursed his own need. How he'd managed to leave behind even his knife—

He answered with a two-note whistle. *Bobwhite!*

Would she recognize it?

Whippoorwill?

He spotted her then, a skirted form with a hunting frock over, as before, pressed against a massive, gnarled oak. Stiffly, he crawled from the cave and stood.

Rifle in one hand, she reached for something behind the tree and stepped out as well. For a long moment they merely stared at each other.

He hadn't told her where he was hiding.

"You said to meet at the rock," he ventured at last.

"I couldn't wait," she said, her voice soft in the predawn gloom. "And I know most of the caves hereabouts, didn't figure it could be so hard to narrow it down." Was it his imagination, or did her lips curve a little? "I hoped the whippoorwill call would help."

He tried a smile in return. "Was that a play on my name?"

She snorted, but the curl of amusement held. "If it is your true name."

Better not to answer that yet.

He looked at the bundle she held. Despite her suspicions, she had come. His eyes burned and he hoped he didn't appear too desperate. Those few bites yesterday had reawakened not just his hunger, but all his hope of life, it seemed.

She stepped forward and gave the bundle a gentle toss toward his feet, then backed away. Still not trusting him, either. "I found a few things that might be helpful."

Micah knelt and tugged at the knot of what he could see now was a wool blanket, worn and much mended. Inside lay a knife, also much used if the nicks of grip and blade were anything to judge by, but the relief of having steel to hand again after losing his own was almost as great as that of the prospect of another meal.

And a meal she'd brought—more johnnycake, with cold roasted venison and an apple, all wrapped in half a handkerchief. His mouth watered, and he took a great bite of the apple. The sweet flavor burst across his tongue.

At the moment, he nearly didn't mind the shame of having admitted to her yesterday that he'd lost everything in his escape from the rebels. Or of having her stand over him as he set the apple aside and tore into the venison.

He glanced up, forcing himself to chew more slowly, then swallow. "My thanks."

She nodded, and apparently convinced he wouldn't turn savage, crouched opposite him, the rifle cradled in her arms. Her eyes were but a glint beneath the brim of her hat. "Have you family?"

Another bite. Chew, swallow. "Two sisters, both married." *A brother, turned rebel. My father, dead of the heartbreak.* "A brother who is a captain of the local militia."

She was very still. "Tories, all?"

He nodded, bit off another mouthful.

"That's all? Sisters and a brother?"

Another nod. "And you? Besides the uncle who's captain of the home guard."

"My father and another uncle rode with Colonel Sevier to hunt Ferguson."

He considered her clothing and the rifle. "And left you to fend for yourself?"

No reply there. He must have hit too close to the truth.

"The settlement is near enough by," she said at

last. "And both of my uncles have families."

He finished the venison and started in on the johnnycakes. She stirred and with the gun stock set against the ground, rose. "I must get back. Wish there was more, but it's all I could spare for now."

"It's—plenty," he said, and meant it. It was more than he'd had at one time since before the battle. "I thank you, again."

Hesitating, she gave a single nod, then took off her hat and held it out to him. "This was an extra. I expect you'll need it."

This one was flat brimmed and plain, he realized, while the one she wore yesterday was cocked.

"Wearing it myself was the easiest way to avoid untoward questions," she added.

Stepping close enough to reach for the hat, he took hold of the brim—and stopped. The morning light caught her eyes and made them a pale blue, soft as a twilight sky. Dark hair, now uncovered, lay caught in a braid that disappeared inside the wide, fringed collar of her coat, but stray wisps curled about her face and framed the angular cheekbones with unexpected softness.

Last thing he'd looked for was her to be so completely fetching.

Eyes widening, she let go of the hat and stepped back. "Well, then. Don't get yourself into too much trouble, now, with that knife."

In a flash, she was gone, darting away between the trees.

Chapter Three

"Why didn't you go back?"

It had been a week since she'd been surprised by the Tory hiding on the mountain, and with each visit, Truth coaxed a bit more of his story out of him—traded food and gear for it, more like. But he didn't seem unhappy about the exchange, though he still hadn't told her his true name.

And today, he'd surprised her by cleaning up. The figure that met her—this time at the hunting rock and not his cave just over the mountain spur—was not the starved, bedraggled one of the first day. He'd put her offerings of well-mended castoff shirt and stockings to use, brushed out his waistcoat, and washed his breeches and hunting frock. His moccasins, though worn and missing laces, were no longer muddy. Most startling of all, however, was finding him clean-shaven with hair combed and tied back, dark eyes watching the forest intently for her approach as she walked up the path.

Only that particular intensity let her know this truly was Will—as well as her father's old hat dangling from his hand and the spare knife stuck in his belt.

And when his eyes lit on her, that strange flutter went through her insides, like she'd felt when he stopped and stared at her the morning she'd given him the hat. He'd gone all still, and his eyes had widened, as if—

Ah, that thought was folly. Hadn't she had her fill of the settlement boys dangling after her? She'd no time for such foolishness, especially not with Papa gone, which ate more at her as the days passed. No more word had come of the battle, except what little she'd gleaned from Will, so she knew not what to expect.

They sat for the moment almost side by side. A fine, clear morning it was, almost warm though a light snow had fallen two days before and melted off. Will chewed at the bone of the turkey leg she'd brought and stared off into the forest, as if he hadn't heard her question. But she knew he had. His quiet was too studied.

He peeled back a piece of the bone and brought it to his mouth to suck the marrow out. "I can't keep taking your charity."

Now, that she hadn't expected, either. He was brighter of eye than even a day or two ago. Surer of hand and step, of a certain.

"'Tis not my intent to sound ungrateful," he went on. "But you hardly need another mouth to feed."

Fear jagged through her chest. What did he know?

He turned his head and met her gaze. "Why did you take pity on me, Truth Bledsoe?"

She swallowed and looked away. "Can't just shoot a hurt, starving critter."

He gave a low laugh. "You can if it deserves shooting."

"Did you?" She couldn't help but stare again.

"I—I ran away." He blinked, but a bitter smile

still twisted his mouth. "Hoped to find death over the mountains rather than face another night hearing the groans of the wounded. Or facing my brother, with this loss on our hands." His chest rose and fell with a breath. "But I'm there again, every night, in my dreams."

She could find no reply to that.

"I'm weary of the fighting. Not a week went by, back home, that someone wasn't getting lynched, or tarred and feathered, or ..."

He fell silent, dragging a hand across his face.

"Well, you've come to the wrong place if you don't like fighting," she said. His dark gaze returned to her, questioning. "Indians," she continued. "Three years ago, it was so bad, they called it 'the Bloody Seventy-seven.'" The reason she was so set on learning to shoot and carry a rifle. "They say the British set the Cherokee against us, because the Crown doesn't recognize our right to settle here."

"And why did you settle here?"

Truth shrugged. "Same as anyone, I reckon. The chance to make a life for ourselves, to work the land and raise a family." They were words Papa had spoken often, but they came alive for her now. "Papa and the others bought the land fairly from the Cherokee. Trouble is, some of their people don't recognize that, either, but we came here by God's grace, and by His grace we'll remain."

Will sat back, frowning. "God's grace," he said, softly. "The loyalist side speaks of that as well. 'Obey the king; he is God's instrument of judgment.' But in the end, whose side is God on?"

How to answer a question like that? "His own, I

expect."

The question haunted her still, once she was home. Scrubbing linens in the washtub in the side yard, boiling them, hanging them out to dry. All she could hear was Will's quiet but impassioned voice, later in the conversation. *Where is the grace in neighbor rising up against neighbor? Men who not five years ago worked alongside each other, helped each other build houses and barns. I cannot go home until I know which side I am willing to lay down my life to defend.*

What was it about him that tugged at her heart? Compelled her to think of how to get him enough food to bring his strength up, to mend the odd castoff item so he could use—

"Hullo the house!" a deep male voice called.

She looked up to see her Uncle Anthony crossing the yard. She straightened the shirt across the rail fence beside the barn, then stepped back, wiping her hands down her blue linen skirt. "Any news of Papa?"

He shook his head.

Who was that man?

In his hiding place on the slope above what he presumed was the Bledsoe farm, Micah shifted for a better look. Three days ago the malaise of starvation had faded enough that he'd crept down the mountain after Truth, for no good reason but curiosity. He hadn't been overly sure as to her identity, the first time she'd walked outside without the hat and hunting frock—especially since a proper cap covered her hair—but the springy, determined stride from house to barn left little doubt. Two other girls were obviously younger, by height, and another girl had flaxen rather than dark hair. He'd also counted only one boy, tallish, but likely too young to be hunting far from the house.

If his guess was right that Truth was the eldest, and her father was off fighting, Micah didn't blame her being so protective of herself and her family.

Now, he watched Truth straighten from her task of washing laundry and greet the rawboned over-the-mountain man approaching with such familiarity. He looked much as the other men at Kings Mountain, and his garb not so different from Micah's and that of other men from the backcountry, but rougher, and hard edged. He wasn't her father, judging by the restraint of her response. More likely her captain-of-the-home-guard uncle.

The man stayed but a short time, conversing with Truth, casting constant glances toward the trees above the house. Micah knew how to remain still and thus unseen.

Even after the man departed, he stayed where he was. Truth's soft words echoed in his mind. *Hospitality is not for repaying.*

And yet—he couldn't not at least try. Especially when, to all appearances, she and her sisters and brother were alone.

Chapter Four

Meeting day. Truth beat eggs into a bowl, measured in handfuls of cornmeal, added milk, and stirred. She'd already warned Will not to expect her today, as they'd be walking to church this morning. It'd be the first time in a while, and she was feeling a longing to be there.

She'd traded with a neighbor, some of her stitching for a ham, and slices of it sizzled in an iron skillet on the coals. Their own hog was ready for butchering, but it wandered the woods until Papa returned. While she stirred the johnnycake batter, she drew a deep breath of the fragrant meat. If there were some left after—not likely with Thomas's appetite of late—she might could slip away up the mountain—

The front door flew open and bounced against the wall behind. Patience stood there, cheeks flushed and chest heaving as if she'd just run half a mile.

A small jolt went through Truth. Was it Indians?

"Who is that man out in the barn, milking our cow?" Patience asked.

Suspicion trickled through her. *He wouldn't!* Truth dropped the wooden spoon against the side of the bowl and pushed it away. "Fry the batter when the ham is done, will you?" she told Patience, then brushed past.

He would, she knew. That obstinate Tory!

Her strides gained fervor until she reached the barn, then mindful of the livestock, she forced herself to not storm inside. Sure enough, a lean male figure in shirtsleeves, with dark hair pulled smoothly back, sat at the cow's flank, milking away as if he belonged there.

In an effort to not fly at him, she leaned back against the sturdy log wall. "I see you know how to milk, at least."

He glanced over his shoulder and grinned, flashing dimples and an impressive set of teeth. Gracious, that wasn't fair. His gaze lingered on her, though his hands never broke rhythm. "There's little difference between a Carolina backcountry cow and an over-the-mountain one, except that the latter's a bit more feisty."

She knotted her hands in her skirts. Idiot man, in *her* barn, and he dared make a joke? "Where did you find the pail?"

He tipped his head toward the corner. "I washed it first, if you're wondering."

"Good thing. I'd hate to waste the milk."

Another grin, then he turned back to the cow.

"Why are you here?"

Senseless question, since she knew already, but she had to ask.

"You need the help."

"We're getting along just fine, thank you."

He tossed another half smile over his shoulder. "That you are. You and—is it three younger sisters and a brother? Or are there more?"

She clenched her teeth on at least a dozen heated

replies, most of which were an insult to his politics, parentage, and character. She must not allow him the upper hand by losing her temper.

"How long have you been watching us?" she said, when she could trust herself to speak civilly.

His milking slowed, as he stripped the last rich drops from the cow. "Three days." Another glance. "Did you expect me to stay in the cave?"

Another deep, long breath. How on earth was she to suffer this insolence? "I'm glad you're better," she said, stammering a little. "But truly—"

He rose, milk pail in one hand, stool in the other, and faced her. His eyes, black in the shadows of the barn, bored into hers. "You're alone. You need help. You've fed and clothed me for a week—now at least allow me to ease some of the burden while your father is gone."

Though soft, his voice left no room for argument.

"And what am I to tell others about your being here?" She fought to keep her own voice from trembling.

"What others? You're not over-close to the main settlement, here. I'd stay well enough out of the way."

"My uncle and aunts. And other folks of the settlement do drop by of an occasion." He didn't move, and she grew desperate. "What of my father when he returns?"

"I can be gone by then."

She shook her head, but he stepped closer. "Please. Put me to work. At least for a few days. I can't bear staying up on the mountain, letting you provide for me while I do naught."

Just as on that first day, something about him caught her. *I know next to nothing about him!* her reason argued. *What is it they were always called—filthy Tories?* But this one hadn't proven himself anything like what she'd been led to believe Tories were. Perhaps his loyalties were misguided, and he could be persuaded to see the right of it. Hadn't he admitted to doubts?

She swallowed but drew herself more straight. "What is your true name, *Will Williams?* Trust me with that, and I'll let you stay."

The dazzling smile appeared again. "Will is good enough for now."

Hissing, she stepped back. Unfortunately, she understood his reluctance to tell her, and she couldn't deny the appeal of a strong back and arms around the farm. Perhaps, since he'd trusted her enough to let her bring him provisions, then followed her home and watched without taking advantage—

She shivered. "Lord help us all. For a few days only, and you'll sleep in the barn."

Was it her imagination, or did relief glint in his eyes? "Fair enough."

A scuff behind her drew her attention, and she turned to find Patience and Thomas standing in the doorway.

"I brought your rifle," Patience said, scooting the weapon into view, "but it don't look like you need it at the moment."

Thomas scratched his nose. "Is he the one you been sneaking away to meet, every morning?"

A groan escaped through gritted teeth as she took the rifle and pushed past them. "Come to the house, and now. We'll be having meeting at home again."

There was no way she'd leave the place under Will's care, however pretty he was, all cleaned up.

Halfway across the yard, she snarled back over her shoulder, "You might as well come too."

At least feeding him would be simpler.

Did she know how magnificent she was when angry?

Micah handed the milk pail off to the girl who, now that he had a good look, was almost certainly the second eldest, but he couldn't help gazing after Truth. A slender thing she was, without the bulk of her hunting coat, but with more than enough fire to make any man want to step down.

And he nearly had, except that he knew her need must be as great as his, in its own way.

The boy lingered by the barn door. His eyes were pale, reminding Micah of Truth's, and a scattering of freckles dusted the boy's nose. "Waiting on me?" Micah asked.

The boy gave a single, grave nod. Micah stowed the milking stool and pointed to the cow. "Do I leave her, or ..."

"Turn 'er out in the pen for now."

Micah nodded, led the beast from her stall, and returned her to the split rail pen adjoining the barn. After, without a word, he followed the boy to the house.

Was that ham he smelled? He was like to drool if he didn't be careful.

Truth was dishing food to the plank table, with the help of the two youngest girls, both of whom peered at him with doubtful blue eyes. Truth herself refused to look directly at him, but after a moment of turning this way and that, she pointed at a bench, near the head of the table. "You. Sit there."

He settled, back to the wall. He'd barely time to glance about the snug interior of the place before she was there again, a stoneware mug in hand. "It's poor excuse for coffee, but it'll have to do. Drink and be welcome, since you're here."

He cradled the vessel in his hands, savoring its warmth, and inhaled. His eyes slid closed. Weak, perhaps, but it was real coffee. He sipped and glanced across to find Truth watching him.

Would he ever be able to repay his debt of gratitude to her?

She nodded toward the boy, standing nearly at his elbow. "This is Thomas. These are my sisters Thankful and Mercy," she indicated the younger girls, "and my sister Patience." A nod toward the girl now bending over the hearth, from whence he caught the definite aroma of corncake. "And this," she went on, "is Will." She hesitated as if to give him time to correct her. "He was, ah, in the battle with Papa earlier this month."

The younger children, but Thomas especially, came alive at that. "A battle! Will you tell us about it?"

He sent a questioning glance toward Truth, and she nodded slightly.

What could he share that wouldn't betray his part in it?

Thomas scooted into the spot beside Micah. "Did they get that rascal Ferguson?"

"Thomas, eat," Truth said. Her gaze flicked to Micah's, guarded.

The girls piled in around the table as well, and Truth slid a wooden plate of food in front of Micah before gracefully seating herself opposite him.

A plate—a real table—how long had it been? Somehow he'd never appreciated it before.

"Did you know Papa?" one of the younger girls asked, shyly. Mercy, he remembered.

Micah shook his head. "I'm from Burke County, North Carolina. Different units." Very different.

"So why are you here, and Papa ain't?" Thomas this time. That boy was as sharp as his eldest sister.

He chewed a bite of his ham. The flavor filled his mouth, and for a moment, all he could think of was his sheer unworthiness to be here.

"Your Papa," he said, when his mouth was cleared, "was with the men guarding the prisoners after the battle." He didn't know for sure—he seemed to remember the name Bledsoe, but couldn't put a face with it. God willing he wasn't of those beating or slashing at the prisoners in their fury and frustration on the march northward. "I was—I was released from duty."

Thomas frowned. "But, if your home is eastward—"

Truth cleared her throat and leaned forward. "God sent him."

Chapter Five

Micah met Truth's eyes across the table. "You believe that." It was more a statement than a question.

"I do." Deliberately, as if daring him to argue, she went back to her food.

"Well then." Micah took up a paring knife and sketched an elongated oval on top of his johnnycake. "This is the top of a place called Kings Mountain, a long, isolated hilltop on the eastern edge of the mountains, roughly west of Charlotte Town."

Thomas and the girls leaned in to watch.

"Here," he pointed to a place near one end of the oval, "is where Ferguson and his men made camp and took their stand. Loyalists all, no British regulars among them but Ferguson himself."

He hesitated. Had he betrayed himself by use of that term, and not "Tory," as the rebel side called them? But no one moved or behaved as though he'd acted amiss.

"Here," and he pointed around the west and south perimeters of the johnnycake map, "your over-the-mountain men climbed, while militia from the backcountry of North and South Carolina and Virginia surrounded from the other. They whooped and hollered, fit to strike terror into the hearts of the Tories, officers and ordinary soldiers alike."

Micah glanced up into the faces surrounding him. Children of one of those men, driven to fury at the threat Ferguson had made to lay waste to their homes with fire and sword.

The chill of those war cries still lodged in his chest, but sitting here among them provided an odd comfort. They deserved to hear the tale of how bravely their father had fought.

"When the loyalists found that their musket fire couldn't match the long rifles, they resorted to bayonets. Three times they pushed their attackers down the mountain, and three times the over-the-mountain men drove them back up, until the loyalists were surrounded and caught in a crossfire from both sides."

Food was forgotten as everyone, Truth included, sat round-eyed. Micah fought to keep his voice level as he recounted what had been the stuff of nightmares every night since. "Some tied handkerchiefs to their musket barrels and tried to surrender, but Ferguson rode the field, swinging his sword and cutting down anyone who raised a white flag."

At Micah's side, one of his cousins had fallen for this very reason.

"At last, as more men surrendered, Ferguson himself tried to leave the field, but he was shot from his saddle and dragged."

"Did he die?" Thomas asked, barely breathing.

Colonel Patrick Ferguson, the Scotsman who rallied the backcountry loyalists as no one else, made the militia into real troops with endless drills and that hated whistle, who'd thought to threaten the over-the-mountain rebels into submission.

Who obviously underestimated the fury that threat would stir.

"He did, indeed," Micah said.

He was quick witted, she'd give him that.

Truth had desperately wanted to stay angry with Will. To not admire the way he'd spun the tale, for her family's benefit and not giving away his own loyalties. But the slight tremor in his voice reminded her of that first day, when he'd begged her not to shoot ...

Please. For the love of God. The battle is over.

She could see him now, surrounded by men trying to surrender. A commander who wouldn't let them. And then—

"Why did you lie for me?"

Will's low voice startled her from her musing. She'd stepped outside after breakfast, and apparently he followed her out.

She rounded on him, but kept her own voice down. "I did not lie."

His eyes narrowed, and a muscle in his lean cheek flexed. "Helping hide me, then. Why?"

A sigh escaped her. "Does it never cross your mind that what I said was, indeed, true? That God directed your path here?"

He stared at her so long, she had to turn away.

"Very well, then," he said. "Put me to work."

~*~*~*~

And work he did, from sunup to sundown, without complaint, without hesitation. Mending the fence on the cow pen, patching the roof on the cabin. Cutting wood, during which Truth made a point of busying herself elsewhere so she'd not be tempted to watch his strong shoulders and arms swinging the axe. More folly—there were fine, manly forms aplenty in the settlements for her to have gone feather-headed over, if she were interested in such. Will would only be here until Papa returned.

But with each passing day, he seemed more at ease. Bantered with Thomas and the girls. Volunteered to fetch the hog from the woods, presided with Truth over setting up the smokehouse and the butchering.

She couldn't remember that task ever being so enjoyable.

Yet, also with each passing day, an unrest gnawed inside her over Papa's whereabouts. Despite Will's assurance that Sevier, Shelby, and the other over-the-mountain men had, best he'd heard, committed to escorting the Tory prisoners to a parole camp north of Charlotte Town, as October trickled into November, and the weather grew colder and more stormy, so did her own worries grow.

She rose from her bed one night, when a nearly full moon shone on the frost, and bundled in a woolen blanket, padded over to peer out the window. She pushed open the shutter just a crack. Icy cold air poured in and swirled around her feet. Across the yard, the roof of the barn glinted in the moonlight.

So far, Will had escaped notice from others in the settlement, but that couldn't continue forever. And then what would she do? Papa was sure to be angry when he returned and found she'd harbored an escaped Tory.

For this past week and more, however, he'd been a Tory no longer. He was simply Will, who had come and somehow made himself needed and necessary.

She didn't know how to deal with him being here—but now, she wasn't so sure she wanted him to leave.

The threat of rain the next morning sent Truth scurrying to make sure enough wood was brought in—although Will had been good about keeping the pile stocked—and to bring in anything that shouldn't be out in the wet. After breakfast, when Will returned to the barn, Truth left Patience in charge of overseeing the younger children's lessons and slipped out after him.

When she entered, he looked up from where he sat on a bench, carving at a piece of wood. "What are you working on?" she asked.

One shoulder lifted. "Something small for Mercy or Thankful. Haven't decided which." He opened his hand to reveal a rough but recognizable cow, emerging from a palm-sized burl of wood. Truth smiled, but he laid aside the carving and the knife. "Did you need aught?"

"Only to bring you this." She pulled a small rolled bundle from beneath her coat and handed it to him.

Bemused, he untied the rawhide thongs binding it, then unfurled two lengths of gray wool.

"Gaiters," she said.

"As if you haven't already done enough." He took one length and wrapped it about his leg, from foot to above the knee.

"Yes, well, you've done more than your share, too." Truth's fingers itched to help with smoothing the gaiter and tying it down, but she could not fathom why. Will was plenty capable of tying his own.

He finished the second in short order and stood, stretching first one leg, than the other. That grin made an appearance. "Very snug. My thanks, as always."

An answering smile tugged at her own lips. "You'll need them. I think I smell snow coming."

He nodded, but absently. "It's about time for your father and the other settlement men to be returning, I'd think."

She clasped her hands behind her back. This was the conversation she wasn't keen on having. But what else was there, but for Will to go? "Will you be returning home?"

A tiny shake of his head. "Not yet." His eyes did not leave hers. "I'm indebted to you, Truth Bledsoe."

Unaccountably, her heart gave an unsteady leap. She swallowed. "You've repaid that debt by now, Will Williams."

A softer smile lighted his lean features, tilted the corners of his dark eyes upward. Had he stepped closer, just then? "Micah," he said.

Her heart was fairly pounding. "What?"

"Micah Elliot. That's my true name. Micah William Elliot."

She mouthed *Will,* then aloud, "Micah."

Closer this time, without a doubt.

"Micah Elliot," she breathed. "It's a good, strong name."

The smile held, as did his gaze. "Would that I were strong enough to be worthy of it."

"I think ... I think you're worthy enough."

Sadness flickered across his face. He touched her cheek. "If you think so ..." Leaving the thought unfinished, he went suddenly still. "How old are you, Truth?"

And why ...? "Eighteen, come the first of the year."

His hand lingering, he gave another little nod, then leaned in. His lips touched hers, held for a heartbeat, then brushed across and were gone.

Will—no, *Micah*—drew back with a look that was at once triumphant and full of wonder. Of their own volition, her hands stole upward to his face and neck, and this time she rose on tiptoe to meet his kiss. Micah gathered her into his arms—

From outside the barn came a male voice, "Halloo the house!"

Chapter Six

"Uncle Loven!" Ignoring her own breathlessness, Truth dashed out of the barn and into the yard, where two horses stood, and a rider dismounted.

The youngest of her three uncles, just a few years older than herself, and the one who'd always seemed more like a big brother. He turned and caught her in a quick hug, which Truth returned despite the grime of his leggings and hunting frock. "My, you're a mess," she said. If only her heart would stop fluttering—perhaps Loven would think it was merely excitement over Papa returning, and not, oh, something else.

He gave her a thin smile. "Fighting Tories will do that to a body."

Another pang of guilt hit her, and she glanced around. "Where's Papa? In the house already?"

Loven took off his worn felt hat, scrubbed his forehead with one sleeve, then shook his head.

Truth shot him a look, but he only gazed back, the pale blue eyes grave.

Two horses, one rider. She turned. Papa's rifle and gear—things he'd normally wear strapped to himself—tied instead to the saddle of his horse.

She opened her mouth, but no sound would come out. A crushing weight caught her chest and would not ease.

"Loven?" she croaked.

He shook his head again. "I'm sorry, girl. There's no easy way to break the news. Your papa took a ball to the side at King's Mountain. The doc said if he didn't move, he had a chance at recovering, but—you know my brother. He insisted on riding with us and took a turn for the worse a week or so ago. We buried him on the way home."

Everything around her blurred, and Truth put out a hand to steady herself against Papa's horse. Loven's hands settled on her shoulders and tugged her toward him. "So sorry, Truth. His last words were for you and the young'uns."

Her sisters and brother. She had to tell them. Had to be strong for them.

And then there was Will—Micah—

Oh Micah.

Oh Lord, how could I?

She pushed away from Loven and stumbled back toward the barn.

Micah saw her coming and held his ground. He'd been listening through the open window, out of sight.

This couldn't end well.

She threw back the barn door and stood, shoulders heaving. Where a few moments ago she'd been all softness, now her grief gave her the fire of an avenging angel.

Not that he blamed her. He'd seen it before.

"Tell me again, please." She took a few steps toward him and stopped. Her voice shook. "Which side of the mountain did you fight on? That south and east end, or—"

He didn't dare touch her this time, though his arms ached to catch her close. "The Burke County militia from both sides were fighting each other. We could hear the over-the-mountain men, but we didn't face them."

At least until later, and he couldn't remember whether he'd gotten off any shots at that point. They were too busy figuring out how to face that wicked crossfire.

Two strides, and she was nearly nose to nose with him. "But how do you know? Do you know of a certain?"

He couldn't help it—he reached for her, his hands cupping above her elbows. But she turned to fury at his touch, shrieking and flinging both fists repeatedly against his chest. "How do you *know,*" she sobbed, nearly incoherent.

Micah closed his eyes for a moment and let her pound on him. "I don't," he said at last.

She gave a wail that lifted the hairs on his neck, and collapsed against him.

To apologize at this moment felt so inadequate. He slid his arms around her, laid his cheek against the linen cap covering her hair, and searched for the words anyway.

With a gasp, she pulled herself upright, eyes red-rimmed, lips trembling. "And I fed you. Gave you clothing and shelter. Oh Lord—*kissed* you—"

One hand over her mouth, she stared at him as if he'd become something awful, then fled the barn.

Past the tall, rawboned man she'd called uncle,

framed in the doorway.

The uncle, who appeared not much older than Micah himself, glanced after Truth, then stepped inside the barn. "How did you think to take advantage of Truth?"

Would to God that Micah's life would not end here, spilled into the floor of Truth's barn. "I was not taking advantage."

"Of a certain you were." The other man strode forward and peered at him more closely. "And I believe I know you."

Micah remembered him as well—oh yes.

Truth's uncle bared his teeth, brows lowering. "You're a filthy Tory, one of those from Kings Mountain. Escaped, did you? What business have you over the mountains?"

No time for dissembling. And if this man had half as much heart as Truth ... "I had—doubts after Kings Mountain. Many of us did. Unlike others, I couldn't return home. One of my brothers had gone rebel, and my oldest brother nearly killed him for it. So I kept running. Next I knew, I was deep in the mountains." He drew a deep breath. "Truth found me one morning while out hunting. She's the one who offered food. The only shred of grace I asked of her was to spare my life. I asked nothing beyond that, I swear."

The hard-eyed man neither moved nor spoke.

"I'm well aware I deserve none of it," Micah went on. "And as for being here—well, I only sought to repay her kindness. It was my intent to leave as soon as her father returned."

"Then do so," Truth's uncle said.

~*~*~*~

Truth sat before the fire, her arms around her younger sisters. Mercy still wept into Truth's skirt, but Thankful had quieted. Beside her, Thomas stared, stony faced, into the fire. Patience was sweeping the floor for what seemed the third time.

Papa would not be returning. She and Patience and the young 'uns were well and truly alone.

And Micah ... it hurt to breathe, at just the thought of him. How could she have been so foolish?

Behind her, the door opened and shut. "Your Tory is packed up and gone," Loven's rumble carried to her.

"He's not my Tory," Truth said.

Thomas sat up, eyes wide. "What Tory?"

Patience had stilled, broom in her hands. "You mean Will?"

"His name is Micah." The words fell from Truth's lips of their own accord. She tightened her embrace around the younger girls.

Thankful squirmed out from under Truth's arm. "How could Will be a Tory?"

Thomas's gaze reflected the fire. "He is not."

Truth's eyes burned. She hadn't wept since returning to the house, and here she was, nearly in tears, over a—a— "He was, yes. What he is now, only the Lord knows."

Thomas's face was very pale. "If he was a Tory, and he was at Kings Mountain, then ..."

Shaking her head, she released Mercy and fled to

the tiny lean-to her parents had shared as a bedroom. With the door shut, she flung herself on the bed, buried her face in the coverlet, and let the weeping come.

Chapter Seven

The cold lay bitter over the mountains, and the red-gold carpet of leaves was fast turning brown. Truth led Thomas and the girls down the well-known path, toward the settlement and toward church, but she glanced upward at the mountain slopes. She had no need to hunt the last few weeks, not with a smokehouse stocked with ham and bacon. And for the better, given the rumor of Indians on the warpath.

She missed her hunting frock and felt hat, but for Sunday meeting, proper won out over practical. A wide-brimmed straw hat covered her cap and a wool cape her gown and petticoats. All was in place, right down to her stays.

Downhill, it wasn't a strenuous walk, and the young'uns chatter should have kept her thoughts busy. But she couldn't help but wonder where Micah was—had he returned home, how long did it take him to get there—or had he stubbornly remained in the mountains? Was he again cold and hungry?

And either way, why did she care?

They arrived at church with time to spare, and inside the log building, Truth herded the family onto their customary bench. Others were arriving as well, but she kept her head down to avoid meeting anyone's eyes. Afterward was the soonest she could face the pitying looks and sad smiles.

The service itself passed in a haze. She usually had little trouble paying attention, but today the words of the hymns and the minister's sermon seemed to slide over her and trickle away like snow melting across the rocky mountainside. She stood when necessary, sat at the appropriate times, kept her hands folded in her lap. Oddly, Thomas and the younger girls managed to hold still as well.

After, they filed out of the building. Outside, where quiet conversation was more acceptable, a trio of women, one older and two younger, stood waiting. Her aunts—Anthony's and Loven's wives—and a cousin.

"Aunt Mary. Sarah. Aunt Milly." Truth greeted them and accepted an embrace from each, in turn.

"Good to see you, dear," Aunt Mary said. "How are you faring?"

The concern in their eyes, as she feared, made her own burn. "Well enough, thank you."

She glanced about to see where the young'uns had gone. Thomas and one of the other boys had run for the edge of the churchyard, kicking leaves in their wake. Thankful and Mercy had a pair of small cousins by the hands and were likewise skipping in the crisp air. Mama would have chided them for it, but Papa would laugh and told her to let them be children while they could.

Milly cleared her throat. "We're a little concerned about you being up there all alone."

"We're just fine, thank you," Truth said.

Aunt Mary pressed in. "You can't honestly be thinking of staying there? Think, Truth—you and the young'uns, through the winter? With threat of—"

She broke off, but Truth could hear the unspoken words. *With threat of Indian attack.* She straightened, pulling her shoulders back. "The smokehouse is stocked. I need some things from the fort, but otherwise, truly, we're fine."

We even have an extra rifle. A tiny sigh escaped her at the thought of Papa's, standing in its corner next to hers.

"How did you get your hog slaughtered?" Aunt Mary asked.

Truth suppressed a wince at the thought of Micah. The image of him, knife in hand, strong and laughing at some sardonic quip she'd made, flashed through her mind. "We had—help."

Aunt Mary's gaze narrowed. "Still. It wouldn't be fitting."

"And whyever not?"

Milly turned. "Loven!" Her youngest uncle was nearly at his wife's elbow already. She looped her arm through his and tugged him closer. "Please tell Truth she and the young'uns can't possibly stay there alone this winter. We could take them in—or Anthony and Mary would be glad to, as well."

Loven's eyes went cool and speculating, his mouth flat—but he held his tongue.

Milly shook his arm. "Tell her!"

"She knows," he said at last, and tugged his wife away.

And he knew entirely too much, himself. Had he told Milly and Mary about her fugitive Tory?

He isn't my Tory, her mind insisted, but her heart

broke afresh.

Papa had lost his life, possibly at Micah's hand—and she'd spared his.

She stirred to find herself standing there alone, or nearly so. Aunt Mary had followed in Milly's wake, and Sarah lingered, but only to talk in low tones to her beau. Truth edged away and headed across the churchyard.

"We gave them just what Reverend Doak said, the sword of the Lord and of Gideon!"

The ringing voice carried from a cluster of men several paces away. Truth halted, her eyes snapping shut. Another ribbon of pain laced across her breast.

"No more than what they deserved," another said.

Oh Papa.

Oh Micah.

How could she feel so torn? She'd heard the threats Ferguson had made, to hang their leaders and lay waste to the settlements with fire and sword, if they did not stay out of the conflict between colonies and Crown.

But Micah was not of that ilk. She knew this.

And yet—if there was the slightest breath of possibility that his hand held the gun that took Papa—

She made herself think of Papa, his last embrace, smelling of leather and bear grease, and his gruff admonition to be strong. The way he'd tucked each of the young'uns in close and whispered to them as well. Perhaps her aunts were right and she should consider moving to one of their farms, at least for the winter. After all, how could she be enough for them all, with him gone?

Almighty Lord, I cannot do this alone ...

"Truth-girl."

She started, but it was only Loven, sidling up to her, and by himself, more's the wonder.

"Of a certain, how are you faring?"

The admission of his concern nearly broke her. She tucked her head, swallowed, and only answered when she thought she could contain herself. "Well enough."

He tipped his head, considering her. "You're not pining over that Tory, are you?"

She'd been right—his pale eyes saw far too much.

"No." It was not a lie. If anything, she pined over her own loss of strength and good sense.

"Good." He chewed the side of his mouth for a moment, glanced over to the other men, still deep in loud reminisce over the battle, then refocused on her. "Was he courting you?"

Her cheeks heated at the memory of what he must have overheard—her admission that she'd gone soft and let Micah kiss her—no, further, had kissed him back. She shook her head. "I think not. It didn't get so far."

He sniffed. "I wonder. 'Tain't like you let anyone try, before. Sooner shoot them as let them talk pretty to you." The corner of his mouth twitched. "You deserve better'n him. And if you're finally of a mind, Joe Greer will be returning soon—"

"I don't want Joe Greer." *Preening peacock.*

"He's at least a real man, not a yellow-hearted

Tory."

She waved a hand, then covered her eyes for a moment. "He didn't run from you, did he?"

Silence, then, "No. He didn't."

Truth waited. He'd have more to say, doubtless.

When it came, his voice was oddly gentle. "I just expected you to have more sense than that, Truth-girl."

She released a long breath. "So did I, Loven. So did I."

With the blade of his knife against stone, Micah struck sparks into the tinder he'd made from shredded bark, then blew them to flame until the twigs he'd collected ignited.

He customarily used coals from the previous fire to start the new, but in his ranging, the fire had been out too long. His tinder, though, was good and dry from being stored off to the side in the cave, and the kindling caught quickly enough. He added a few smaller pieces of wood then sat back, tipping his head to scan the sparkling, rippled surface of the cave ceiling. The rear part of the cave was damp, with a passage leading downward to a stream, but here, the floor remained dry and sandy.

Inside the low opening, the cave was wide enough for a man to stand up comfortably and deep enough for several to find shelter. And unlike during his early days here, he was one blanket richer, along with one knife, one hat, and assorted proper gear.

All in thanks to Truth.

Why he could not simply cross back over the mountains and head for home was a mystery. She'd made it clear enough that he was no longer welcome—and he blamed her not a whit. But something compelled him to stay. Whether it was because he'd left his heart down at that farm at the mountain's foot, or something else, he couldn't say.

Did staying still make him a coward?

He let his mind play back over the past few years since the war's outbreak. It hadn't seemed to touch them much in North Carolina. A few skirmishes here and there, neighbors snarling at each other over fences—until the British firmly took Savannah and Charles Towne and started their push into the backcountry. Then men's blood truly began to boil.

He was weary of it, truth be told.

When the fire was warm enough, he lit a torch he'd made from mosses and took himself down the rear passage to the stream. Being careful to not slide on the rocky bottom, he bathed and then washed out his shirt and breeches.

Shivering afterward—though the temperature of the cave was constant, and far warmer than outdoors, it was still cool to his bare, wet skin—he made his way back to the fire to dry himself and his clothing.

The welts and deep bruises of two months past were faded now, except for the occasional ache in his ribs. He stretched, pulling on the shirt, then held the breeches out toward the flames. He'd swam the creek many a time, even in the cold, and tramped the countryside with wet clothing, but taking the edge off the damp would certainly make them more comfortable.

The thought of home pricked at him. Christmas was near. Did his sisters wonder what had befallen him, and mourn? Did John care a whit that his absence might cause them pain, or did he merely curse and rave at Micah's disappearance, certain that another brother had gone rebel?

And then—the image of Truth, with her wry smile and light grey eyes, flashed before him. The younger children, shy but laughing. Christmas couldn't be aught but a gloomy affair for them. And what if that was indeed his fault? Truth's wild grief at that possibility chilled him even now.

Even now, he could feel the softness of her lips, of her slight form as for that moment, she'd yielded to his embrace.

Just for a moment, but it was enough. He'd never be the same after kissing Truth.

A kiss was not sufficient, however, to erase the horror of where he'd been, that her father could have met his end at Micah's hand.

All the more reason my life should be spent making up for that loss.

The strength of that thought stole his breath. His eyes snapped shut. A lifetime at Truth's side—providing for her, protecting her—nothing until now had seemed as worthy a cause to spend himself upon.

But could she be persuaded to see it thus? And would she ever forgive him for being in the wrong place at the wrong time?

Chapter Eight

Micah went steadily but as silently as he could through the twilight, across the slopes that would take him back to the cave. After being here for more than a month, he could find his way in the near-dark with little trouble. He'd ranged far today, and the last glow from the sunset had faded as the first stars glittered above, leaving the mountains in crisp, bitter cold. His snares had netted him a pair of rabbits—lean as far as meat went, but at least he'd not starve again, yet.

As he picked his way through the laurel and around a fall of boulders, an owl's hoot broke then stillness, then another. At the third one, from a different direction, he stopped. A chill brushed his skin, lifting the hairs on the back of his neck.

He slid into a man-sized crack between the boulders. The owl hoot came again, closer. Forcing his breathing to shallowness, he waited. Muscles cramped, and skin prickled.

Voices, low at first, then rising in agitation. Micah caught a few words—Cherokee, if he didn't mistake what his brother had taught him, with English mixed in.

Settlements. And, *warpath.*

Micah's blood turned to ice in his veins.

Was he understanding them aright? What if his memory served them wrong and they were merely talking of a hunt?

On the other hand, what Indians hunted ordinary prey at night, well after sunset?

The voices fell silent, and he held himself still, barely breathing. There was a rush, as of a wind sweeping through the winter-bare trees. Micah peeked out, and the dark shapes of two or three dozen bodies, perhaps more, streamed past the boulders. Downhill, and definitely toward the settlement.

And between here and there lay Truth's farm.

Micah waited until the last echo of the war party—if it was such—had faded, then he slid out of his hiding place, considered his direction, and took off down the mountain as well.

Young'uns tucked in bed, at last. Truth listened to the last shuffling sounds of Thomas and the girls in the loft above as shawl-wrapped, she made her rounds, padding from door to windows, making sure all was shut and barred.

Of late, this was the moment she most looked forward to, all day. The house quiet, the young'uns settled, and the first breath of rest since she lifted her head from the pillow that morning. She couldn't remember it ever being this hard before, but then—she'd always had Papa's return to look forward to, before.

No longer.

She paused at one window, fingertips on the barred shutter. If not for the cold, she'd open it and just stand there, soaking in the evening's peace. Tonight, a shiver ran through her, and she turned away.

Sighing, she rubbed a hand across her face. It would be Christmas in just a few days. Memories assailed her of Mama and Papa, gathering them all by the fire for a reading of Scripture, the house fragrant with roast bird and pie and sweets that Mama had labored over for what seemed like days. There'd be no more of that for the young'uns, unless she made the effort. She had enough sugar for a small cake, but she'd have to borrow cream and eggs from Aunt Milly. Her own cow had gone dry a couple of weeks ago and would not come fresh now until early spring.

They could have a very decent day of it, if none of them dissolved into tears as had been their habit of late ...

A thumping on the front door drew a gasp from her lips and spun her around. Who might—?

"Truth! Open up, it's Micah."

Heart pounding, she flew to the door, then reached for her rifle before she lifted the bar. Fumbling, she pulled it open. The wild man who stood there, hat in hand, illuminated in candle and firelight—bearded, hair mussed, eyes wide—minded her again of that first day. And once again, she could hardly move. "Micah?"

His name escaped her throat in a squeak.

"There's no time—may I come in?"

She stepped back, and he did so, shutting the door behind him. His gaze fastened on hers, every bit as intent as she remembered.

"Indian attack," he said, breathless. "I came to warn you."

She put out a hand, and he gripped her arm, steadying her.

"The settlement," she gasped.

"Aye. I'll go." He tipped his head, gesturing with his free arm, and for a moment his mouth flattened in what looked like a rueful half smile. "I know the way. Been scouting about this past month."

Heat flashed through her. He hadn't left. He'd stayed ... but why?

The cold took her again, and she found herself trembling.

His gaze swept the room before coming back to her. "I'll be back as soon as I can. Just—stand ready." A definite smile this time, sweet and tender and heart-piercing. "I know how well you can use that rifle. Give 'em fire if they're here before I return."

Then he was gone, the door shutting behind him with a solid thud. Truth shook herself and set the bar back in place.

Whirling, she stared about her. So much to be done. But first—

She went to the table and blew out the candle. Then at the fireplace, she set aside the rifle and dropped to her knees. With the poker, she spread the logs apart so the flames would die more quickly to embers.

And there she lingered, in prayer for the young man she'd sent away, but who'd somehow returned to warn them all of danger.

To her amazement, the house stayed quiet.

~*~*~*~

Micah's lungs burned from the cold, but still he ran, across the fields undoubtedly cleared and worked by Truth's father, through a stand of thick timber, down a ravine. He dodged mossy boulders and leaped a narrow, swift stream, still gurgling despite the recent freeze. In the dark, his foot slipped, went down in a pool so cold his foot was instantly numb, but he scrambled up and kept going.

The lingering fear for Truth and her sisters and brother nipped hard at his heels, making the short distance to the farm of Truth's uncle seem miles longer than he knew it to be.

If there had been anyone else closer, Micah would go there, but it made more sense to warn her uncle first—even if it was the youngest, Loven, rather than the hard-faced oldest.

Micah only hoped the man wouldn't shoot him on sight.

He'd barely reached the next set of harvest-bare field before a hound bayed somewhere ahead of him. He set his teeth and put on a last burst of speed. The baying became more urgent.

Halfway across the field, he slowed. "Ho the house!"

A door opened, silhouetting a man in shirtsleeves, holding a rifle. He gave a low command, and the baying subsided to a growl and whine. "Who is it?" the man called.

"A friend." Heaving for breath, Micah walked to the edge of the porch, where the light touched him, and leaned his hands on his knees for a moment.

"You," the man grunted.

Micah lifted his head, then straightened. "Aye, it's me. Shoot me if you wish, but I came to warn you, there's what looks like a war party of Indians headed this way."

Loven Bledsoe's head came up, apparently searching the darkness behind Micah. He beckoned Micah inside.

The man's wife stood near the fire, still poised in shock. Micah dipped her a quick bow, then turned back to Truth's uncle. "Thirty or forty braves met together, then passed me up on the mountain. I overheard them talking—fairly certain they mean to attack, although my Cherokee's a bit rusty."

"Well." The iron set of Loven's jaw did not ease, but he put down the rifle and reached for his hunting frock, hanging behind the door. "We're too far from the fort to take refuge there, but I'll need to spread the word. Did you warn Truth?"

Micah sucked in another deep breath, grateful for the warmth of the snug cabin. "Went there first."

Loven gave a quick nod and buckled his belt around the coat. His gaze flicked over Micah. "And you're going back, I expect?"

"I am. She and the children shouldn't be alone."

"Somethin' we agree on," Loven muttered, reaching for his hat. He held one arm out to the woman, who stepped close for a quick kiss and embrace. "Bundle yourselves and the young'uns, follow him over to Truth's." Another glance at Micah. "You'll not mind?"

"I'd be honored," Micah said.

Chapter Nine

Truth heard the voices before the soft scratching came at the door. She opened to find Milly and her two young'uns standing outside. Behind them, Micah was tying a huge dog to the corner of the porch.

Her heart did a strange flutter. "Loven let Micah bring Brutus?"

Milly flashed a smile. "The hound is useful for sounding alarm." She stepped past Truth to the lean-to bedroom, leading the bundled little boys.

Finished with the dog, Micah stood back, hat in hand, his expression lost in shadow. "Get inside," Truth whispered, and barred the door after him.

She took his hat and hung it on a peg beside hers. She'd not think about how Papa's hung there day after day.

Loven trusted Micah with his hound ... and his wife and young'uns ...

Micah stood there, entirely too close. She twitched away, reached for Papa's rifle and thrust it into Micah's hands. "Here." She kept her voice low, but it sounded harsh in the stillness. "Make yourself useful. Can you reload, or should I set Milly to do it for you?"

She knew without looking that his bearded mouth would be curling in a grin. "My older brother has a fine Pennsylvania longrifle. I've handled it a time or two."

"That'll do, then." She handed him a shot bag—she'd counted more than twenty balls—and a powder horn.

Both Papa's. Again, she'd not think about it.

He huffed the breath of a laugh. "Where do you want me?"

She pointed at the window to the left of the door. "There. Reckon we'll have to unbar the windows to properly keep watch."

With a nod, Micah moved into position. Truth watched him for a moment as he opened the window, then with quick movements, slung the pouch and powder horn straps over his body, and between glances outside, counted the balls. "Is this all you have?" he said, hushed.

"I've an equal amount saved back." She swallowed. "Will the Indians head straight for the settlement, do you think, or burn houses and farms as they go?"

He gave a little shake of his head. "Hard to say. They'd have been here by now if they intended to hit as they go. Doesn't mean the danger's over, though."

Milly came, rustling softly, from the lean-to. "I've put the boys to bed. What do you need me to do?"

Truth considered. "There's a small window near the bed. You could keep watch there, whistle if you hear anything amiss."

Milly hesitated, glanced toward Micah. The curiosity must be burning inside her, but they must not make idle conversation. "We have water?"

"Enough 'til morning, at least."

And if they did not survive until then—it wouldn't matter.

Milly whisked away to the back room.

Truth carried a stool to her chosen post, placed it carefully, and eased open the shutter where not an hour ago she'd stood. Peering out now was a different matter entirely, but with a gust of cold, only the deep quiet of evening greeted her. A sullen quiet, it seemed.

She exchanged her shawl for hunting frock, and slipped her own shot pouch and powder horn into place, slung across her body. She'd already removed her cap and stowed it in her pocket, so as not to make more of a target than they already were. With rifle leaning upright against her shoulder, she settled onto the stool, a little back from the window.

Were they out there even now, waiting? She suppressed a shudder. Her own grandfather had disappeared in the wilderness, fallen presumably at the hand of some Indian brave. She nearly couldn't visit the merchants at the fort without hearing talk of Indian attack, with the horrors of being scalped or captured described in detail.

Papa had often said that he and his brothers had moved further out on the frontier to escape government interference and political squabbling, but which was worse? The Cherokee remained as divided as any over the white men's land purchases this side of the mountains.

And yet, this was the life she knew. She wanted naught else, unless it was to have Papa back, and Mama. And, God willing, someday a family of her own.

Her eyes strayed across to Micah. She could just see the outline of his form beside the open window. Feet set apart, shoulders wide under the fringed double collar of the hunting frock. Dark hair loose over that, the hint of a strong brow and straight nose as he gazed out into the night.

Her throat tightened. Why did he agitate her so? Was it merely the knowledge that Micah was there—where Papa took the musket ball that later took his life—and could have been the one to deliver it? Or was there more?

God sent you.

Her own words haunted her.

As if she'd spoken aloud, Micah turned his head, meeting her gaze in the dark. Neither of them moved.

~*~*~*~

Even in the dark, he could see the hint of curls around her face. His memory filled in the tilt of her cheekbones and chin.

Did she despise the necessity of him being here? Or was that spark he'd seen in her eyes, when she'd first opened the door to him, one of relief and gladness? 'Twould be easy enough to imagine it as such. Too soon to tell whether she tolerated his presence simply because she needed him to fire a rifle if the Indians attacked.

Which he should be watching for, instead of letting her distract him.

He turned back to the window. All was quiet,

including that great hound Loven had insisted he bring along. Not that he was ungrateful—as Loven's wife had said, the dog would be useful to raise an alarm should anything happen.

And Truth's expression of surprise had warmed him clear through.

He stole another glance at her, but she'd returned to looking outward as well, perfectly still and straight, one hand curled around the barrel of that rifle.

Brave, fetching girl. He had so much to say to her if they lived through this night.

Please, Almighty God. I'm not in the habit of praying anymore, but—protect and spare her. Protect these people.

And—if I did shoot the ball that took her father, I ask that you pardon my soul. Did we not all only do what we felt was right?

Only the silence echoed back to him, but a small measure of ease filled his heart.

The night wore on. A distant wolf howled, then an owl hooted. The hairs on Micah's neck raised again. He lifted the rifle, held it half at ready, but nothing stirred nearby. The hound growled, but only the once.

A creaking came from the ladder to the loft. Truth's next youngest sister, Patience, descended and tiptoed over to her. They whispered briefly, then Patience went to the pail on the table, dipped a tin cup of water, and brought it to Micah. He nodded his thanks and drank it down.

After he handed back the cup, Patience stood there like she wanted to say something to him as well. Micah glanced at her, but after a moment she returned to Truth's side.

The next hour or two passed without event. Micah reckoned it to be close to midnight, and he scrubbed at his face in the attempt to stay awake.

Truth sidled up to him, her presence more felt than heard. "Think we dare sleep? If Brutus will bark or growl ..."

He shrugged. The temptation to sleep was strong, but the later the hour, the more likely the Indians would double back from their planned target. And if the two of them weren't both awake, ready to respond the moment of attack, could they hold them off?

"Been thinking," he murmured. "If they come, we should do all we can to make it seem there's more than two of us."

"We could take turns firing and loading, moving from one window to the other."

"Should work." He forced himself to sound calm, but just having her standing there, elbow nearly touching his, set all his senses at ready. It wasn't sleep he wished to dare, suddenly, but to tuck her into arms again, and—"Do you have more than the two rifles? An old musket at well, perhaps?"

"No. But I have Papa's tomahawk and hunting knife, if need be."

A smile tugged at his mouth. "You'd be right fierce with either of those, I expect."

She huffed softly—was that a laugh, for his benefit, or merely derision? He let himself look at her. Between the pert nose and chin, her mouth was firm, all outlined in shadow.

"I'm going to feel mighty foolish if this turns out to be for naught," he said.

At that, she turned, her gaze catching his. "Don't."

Her eyes widened, as if she'd just admitted something she didn't want him to know. Her lips parted and shut, and she glanced away. He imagined, if there were enough light, he would have seen her flush.

"I—I was over-harsh with you, weeks ago, that day when Loven came home," she said. "You couldn't have known—"

She broke off, half turned away. He reached out and caught her arm, but gently. "The news of your papa was a terrible shock."

Her eyes glimmering, she looked up again. He let his fingers slide down her sleeve until they closed over her hand.

"If I could bring him back to you," he said, "I would. If somehow I could go back there and exchange myself for him ..."

Her grip tightened on his. "Don't—not that, either. 'Tain't fitting to question what God has decreed."

For a long moment, they stood almost nose to nose, unmoving. "It isn't questioning God to admit you grieve," he said. "I remember what it's like to lose a mother and father. And if it pains you that I'm here and your papa isn't, well, no one can blame you for that."

She drew a soft, uneven breath. Then, tough over-the-mountain girl that she was, she sagged against him, forehead to his shoulder.

Outside, the hound shot to his feet, baying.

Chapter Ten

Truth sped back to her window. Her eyes strained through the darkness—was that movement at the far corner of the barn? If Brutus's continued baying was any indication, yes. She raised the rifle and sighted.

Micah was at her shoulder. "The hound's pointed toward the cow pen. Could be there, and maybe beyond the house a little. Don't fire just yet, until you're sure what it is."

An unearthly shriek split the night, chilling Truth to the marrow. She remembered that cry from the night in the fort, three years past. "I'm sure," she said, and pointing the rifle at the nearest flicker, just beyond the rail fence, squeezed the trigger.

The boom of the gun shook the house as the rifle stock kicked against her shoulder. The acrid smell of burnt powder filled her nostrils. She stepped back to let Micah take position and up-ended the rifle for reloading while thumbing open the powder horn. A measure of powder, tipped down the barrel, then a patch and ball from inside the pouch on her other side. Ramrod out, then—

A flash and a blast heralded Micah's shot. She had the ball and patch tamped nearly down the barrel. Micah slid to the wall opposite her and began reloading as well.

Ramrod back in place. Truth lifted the rifle,

primed the pan with a slight dusting of powder, dropped the horn and swung the rifle to her shoulder again. More shrieks, overlaid with Brutus's frantic yips and howls.

"Wait," came Micah's voice, steady and low. "Wait ... and ... there."

Movement accompanied the nearest-sounding war cry. She pointed and fired again. Stepped back. Tipped up rifle, powder horn in hand.

Lord in heaven, preserve us! She had twenty or so balls, and plenty of powder. Could they hold off a full-scale attack?

And how many times had Papa and her uncles and the other men faced battle? Had Papa felt this white-hot determination to fight until last breath?

Ramrod down ... next to her, Micah fired again and moved aside. She slid the rod into place, primed the pan, stepped into place.

She mustn't waste balls. *Oh God, let me shoot true. For my sisters and brother. For Milly and the boys—*

A flash from past the barn betrayed return fire, and Truth heard the ball hit somewhere beside the open window.

Squeeze the trigger. Flame and smoke, and the kick against her shoulder. Move back and reload again.

A thin cry—one of the girls—came from above, then was drowned by the roar of Micah's next shot.

Ramrod down—down—this ball was stubborn—

The cry was muffled now.

Micah reloaded, glancing out the window. Truth slid the ramrod home and stepped up.

Milly came scurrying out of the back room. "There's more," she panted, "behind the house."

Micah darted away before Truth could move. She gritted her teeth, torn between the desire to just shoot and the knowledge that she mustn't just blaze away into the night. Every shot counted. But now—

The thunder of Micah's rifle echoed from the tiny lean-to. One of the boys yelped—likely Isaac, the youngest.

How long before the Indians figured out that it was just the two of them shooting, and made their attack in that precious half-minute while they were reloading?

She searched for movement. Brutus' baying changed in pitch—was he pointed another direction? She leaned to one side to see back past the porch—there, a flash and boom, and a shutter at the other window exploded in splinters.

Without thought, Truth raced across the room, lifted the gun and sighted. She fired then ducked back to reload.

A flurry of shouts echoed from the field beyond the barn, then the crackle of gunfire echoed after. The settlement men, in pursuit of the war party?

Or reinforcements for the attack?

Her breaths came in gasps. The next moments would tell. As a second boom rolled across the cabin from the lean-to, she made her hands continue the task—ball, patch, ramrod. Slide the ramrod back into place—sidestep to the window, rifle to her shoulder.

Oh Lord ... merciful Lord ...

A few more shots rang out. The war cries

seemed to scatter and fade. Truth waited, still at the ready. Behind her, someone scuttled up the loft ladder—mostly likely Milly. Patience had gone back to bed hours ago.

"Halloo the house!" came a call, as Brutus's baying quieted to a yelp and a growl.

Truth sagged against the wall and closed her eyes.

Micah made sure their attackers were on the run, then with the barest glance toward the two boys huddled on the bed, he left the back room and crossed to where Truth leaned, rifle cradled in her arms. He set a hand on her shoulder, and her eyes fluttered open.

"It wasn't for naught," she said, and he shook his head slowly.

"Truth, be you there?" The deep voice of one of her uncles carried through the open window.

She pushed upright and glided past him to the door. The rawboned man outside wasn't Loven, but the older one he'd seen speaking to her weeks before. She threw herself into his embrace. "Uncle Anthony!"

"Is everyone safe?" His gaze swept the room, came back to Micah with a sternness that made Micah think he might be better off facing the Cherokee.

Loven's wife and Patience descended the ladder, followed by the younger children. "We're all well," Loven's wife said.

The two boys spilled out of the back room. Half the children aimed for Truth and her uncle, but Thomas, Thankful, and Mercy all surrounded Micah. "Will!" Mercy exclaimed, and launched herself at him.

He caught the girl in a quick hug. The other two hung back a little, eyeing him uncertainly. Thomas lifted his chin. "It's Micah now, Truth said."

He let out a rueful laugh. "Will is part of my middle name."

Thankful still glared. "Why did you leave without sayin' farewell?"

"Are you back to stay?" Mercy chimed.

He shook his head. "I only came to warn the settlement about the Indian attack."

Amid the girl's expression of disappointment, Truth's uncle, who'd apparently been listening to the exchange, looked pointedly at Micah and cleared his throat. "I'm following the chase up the mountain. You coming? We could use another rifle."

Micah checked his gear and reached for his hat. Truth made to come as well, but Anthony Bledsoe shook his head. "You stay here with the young'uns. Just in case."

Her shoulders dropped like a chastened child's, but Micah thought she didn't look as disappointed as she might.

The night had been harder on her than she wished to let on, he guessed.

As her uncle slipped outside, Micah stopped and caught Truth by the elbow. "I'll be back later."

Her lips thinned, but she gave a quick nod, then

glanced away. Throwing herself into his embrace as she had her uncle's would have been more encouraging, but—there was no helping it for the moment.

Out into the clear cold, he followed, running after the war cries echoing down from the mountainside timber above.

They gave chase, some on horseback and some on foot, until dawn began to lighten the skies. At last, the other men agreed that the Cherokee were long gone, and it was safe to return to their homes. Some stayed out to keep watch, and Micah accompanied the rest down to the valley's edge.

Not far from Truth's farm, they stopped, gathering in a rough circle. Loven had already told the others of Micah's part in sounding the alarm. Thanks and handshakes were offered from all around, while Loven smirked knowingly from a short distance. Some of them, like Loven, Micah recalled by face from those long days as a prisoner after the battle. Being back in their company, greeted as an equal, at the edge of deep forest where his arms couldn't but half span the biggest trees, and where just hours earlier the war whoops of Indian and white man had echoed—it was eerily like Kings Mountain, and yet unlike.

When the other men had said their farewells and gone, Loven Bledsoe lingered behind. Anthony had gone with those riding patrol for the day. "Since I need to go collect Milly and the boys," Loven said, "I'll walk with you down to Jacob's place."

Truth's father's name. Micah hesitated, but Loven beckoned to him and set off. The man's long, braided hair swung across his back as he walked.

Micah trotted to catch up.

"No use pretending that ain't where you're headed next." Loven glanced over. The look in his pale eyes was so reminiscent of Truth, it made Micah's throat ache. "Wonder how many of those young bucks will be after your hide when they find out you aim to marry her."

Micah wondered that himself, but he wouldn't say so to her uncle. "If she'll have me."

Loven snorted. "She's gone terrible soft where you're concerned, make no mistake about it." He stopped and swung toward Micah, studying him with a frown. "Why did the young'uns call you Will?"

"It's what I went by, when Truth first found me. My middle name. Didn't want anyone to know who I was, where I'd come from."

"And you are ...?"

"Micah Elliot. Lieutenant in the militia, Burke County, North Carolina."

Loven's expression remained still. "And you think you can make a life here, over the mountains?"

Micah lifted one hand, palm upward, then let it fall. "There's a girl down there what makes me want to try."

Another long look. Loven blew out a breath. "If you ever hurt Truth—"

He straightened, met Loven's eyes with a stern gaze of his own. "I'd never intentionally hurt her. Never."

The ghost of a smile crossed the other man's

mouth. "Well. See to it, then."

And he set off walking once more.

Chapter Eleven

Truth ignored the quivering in her limbs as she and Milly led the young'uns in all the ordinary things that needed doing after such a night—fetching water and wood, tending spooked livestock, mending the broken shutter, emptying chamber pots. The attack had passed hours ago, and now all that was left was the weariness, and the need to keep moving, lest she fall asleep on the spot.

One of the young'uns gave a cry, and she turned to see Loven striding across the yard. Milly ran to meet him, she and their boys, and not until they closed about him did Truth notice who followed after.

Micah.

He tipped his head, watching her from beneath the brim of his hat, not smiling but walking with purpose. Toward her.

For some odd reason, she could not move. Last night, she'd found herself weakening toward him again, but today, in daylight, things seemed more difficult. He slowed as he neared her, as if he felt it as well.

"We saved you some breakfast," Milly said, addressing Loven, but turning to include Micah.

"You're welcome to stay and eat," Truth murmured, her gaze never leaving Micah's.

He half smiled and dipped his head toward

Milly, then removed his hat. "If it'd be no trouble."

But when Loven and Milly and the young'uns all continued toward the house, he didn't follow.

Truth's chest felt strangely tight as Micah studied her, long-lashed dark eyes narrowing, one hand raking back his hair. All at once, she remembered her manners. "I thank you, for what you did last night."

The lashes fell, and he shook his head, mouth curving slightly. "It's I what should thank you, for giving me back my life."

Sensible thought fled. She'd only done what she felt compelled to, by Christian charity.

She'd not admit it had become far more than that.

Head tilted, he looked at her again. "Truth Bledsoe, I have something I need to say to you, so hear me out. Recall when I told you I wouldn't decide about returning home until I found something worth laying my life down for?"

The intentness of his gaze begged a reply, and she gave a quick nod.

"Well, I've found it. It's you, sweet Truth. I'd gladly spend the rest of my life as I did last night—standing beside you, defending you. That is, if—" He went shy, shifted from one foot to another, cradling Papa's rifle in his arms. "If you'd be willing."

His gaze became direct again. "You need the help, you and the girls and Thomas. But I'll not make a pest of myself, or demand an answer before you're ready to give it. You take your time, and when you've decided, you know where to find me."

The fine morning blurred before her eyes, and she could not speak for the thickness of her throat. Blast him, what was this he did to her?

If it pains you that I'm here, and your papa isn't …

She blinked, swallowed, tried to speak.

He smiled a little, then held out the rifle. "It's a fine piece," he said softly, and once her hands closed about it, took off the shot pouch and powder horn and handed those to her as well. "My thanks for the use of them."

She fumbled with the straps, but he curled her fingers around them. He hesitated, then leaned in, lips pressing to hers and lingering for but a moment.

He smelled like the wild forest.

In the next moment, he backed away. "It was a long night. Rest soon."

And then he was gone.

Could she walk back into the cabin and pretend nothing was amiss? Her feet carried her there, regardless. Inside, she sank onto a stool and simply sat there, while Milly and Loven stared at her.

"Well," Loven said. "That didn't end as I expected."

"Isn't he staying for breakfast?" Milly said.

"No," Truth said.

"What happened?"

Truth blinked. Her sister-in-law's gentle but probing tone brooked nothing short of a reply. "He asked me—" What exactly had he asked, anyway? Of a certain, something far more than *let me sleep in your barn and fix your fences.* He'd said the words "for the rest of my life."

"He asked me to marry him," she said, and buried her face in her hands.

It felt like the whole cabin stopped to hear what she'd said.

"Oh Truth," Milly said.

"And—do you want to?" Loven asked.

She made herself breathe—in and out—then pressed her hands to her knees and looked at them. Patience stood on the other side of the table, as well, poised to listen.

"How can I marry him and not be untrue to Papa?"

The silence was broken only by the laughter outside of the young'uns at play.

Loven's gaze was steady. "Your papa would want you to do whatever is best for you and the young'uns."

"And that would be—?"

He let out a long breath. "It's my thought that what took place at Kings Mountain is best left there."

Something Micah had said pricked in her memory. "And what of—what took place after?"

Was it her imagination, or did Loven flinch, just a little? He swallowed. "That too. Our rage was slow to die, Truth-girl. But Ferguson threatened our homes and families, and the threat of the Cherokee has been hard enough without the Crown trying to bully us directly. Micah understands that now. Think of what he risked to come down here last night to warn us."

What he had risked—to defend her. The words wrapped her about.

But Papa ... Papa would have tanned her hide if he'd thought she'd gone soft over a Tory.

"I just don't know." She rose and turned toward the back room. "I'm tired. Patience, wake me up long about noon, will you?"

Days later, she still didn't know.

It was Christmas Eve. A sudden snow kept them from going anywhere, so Truth had sat the young'uns down for the traditional reading from Scripture. As she turned to the familiar passage about a cold night and a passel of frightened shepherds visited by angels, the pages kept falling open to other places, and the odd sentence would leap to attention. *But love ye your enemies, and do good, hoping for nothing again ... be ye therefore merciful, as your Father also is merciful.*

If your enemy hungers ...

Her hands stilled on the pages. She'd given of what she had, not expecting a reward—and God had been merciful in sparing their lives.

God sent you ...

What if He truly had sent Micah to be more to her?

She pressed ahead to the Christmas passage. *Fear not: for behold, I bring you good tidings of great joy ... on earth peace, good will to men.*

And further down, *...mine eyes have seen thy salvation.*

Hours after, she could not sleep. The cabin was quiet, but as her habit in the nights since the attack, she couldn't seem to settle. She lay in her bed and listened to the howling wind, and wondered for the hundredth time where Micah was. Closing her eyes, she let herself think about his mouth on hers, the warmth of his breath on her cheek, those dark eyes and his dimpled grin. The kiss in the barn—again. The feel of his arms around her for that moment, lean and strong, and his shoulder beneath her cheek.

She rose from her bed, wrapped a blanket around herself and pushed her feet into worn fur-lined moccasins, then paced the main room as soundlessly as she could.

Salvation, through the hand of a Tory. Was that so difficult to believe? For some, perhaps. She knew—and others as well, she'd heard Loven and Milly speaking of it—that it was salvation from the hand of God. Not only on that night so recently passed, but—for the span of their lives, through that Child born so long ago.

Forgive us our trespasses, as we forgive those who trespass against us.

She dropped onto a chair, weeping.

Lord in heaven, can I forgive? And if I do not, how can I, in turn, merit your great grace?

She did not merit it, then or now. Else it was not grace.

Chapter Twelve

Truth peeked out through the shutter as the sky held the colors of a newborn day. The overnight snowstorm left everything covered in glittering white. Each tree branch and twig bore its own delicate coating, minding her of lace or sugar glaze.

She'd finally returned to bed, and lulled at last by the relative safety of snow and wind, slept until just about dawn, when she awoke with a fresh sense of purpose and a strange, sharp joy.

Patience tiptoed up to peer out as well. Truth opened her blanket, offering to share the warmth. The younger girl nestled against her side, and Truth tugged the blanket around them both.

"It's beautiful," Patience breathed.

"It is, that. Merry Christmas, little sister."

Patience giggled. "Merry Christmas."

Thomas popped up on their other side. "Shall I fetch the ham now?"

He was getting near as tall as her, she noted. "Hmm, in a bit. First, I want you to run over and let Uncle Loven know that we won't be coming to church or dinner today."

Both Patience and Thomas stared at her, but she only smiled. "Shoo now. I have other plans brewing, but don't tell them that."

Thomas dashed off to finish dressing. With a regretful sigh, Truth closed the shutter and set

Patience to build a fire. They'd not be here long, but the front room was ice cold.

In the lean-to, which she'd been making her own after the news of Papa's death, she lingered over the decision of what to wear. The odd desire to look her best warred with the need for practicality—but she'd be climbing the mountain today, after all. Over her shift, she tied on a set of jumps rather than the boned stays. Over that, her pocket and two layers of petticoats, a quilted calico first, then the faded indigo she usually wore. Her red and blue flowered shortgown went next—it had been one of Mama's—and the knitted elbow-length mitts she was never without during the colder months. And under, of course, went stockings and leggings and moccasins.

Her cap, however—she tucked that into her pocket, after brushing and braiding her hair. She would not be tramping up the mountain in a mere hood and cape, if she could help it.

Out in the main room, she gathered what they'd need—the frame for the iron spit, half a dozen small pumpkins for roasting, sugar and spices folded carefully into a clean cloth, the dried berry pie she'd baked the day before similarly wrapped. Their great Bible, in its own carrying pouch. All of it, settled carefully into haversacks and blanket-bundles for carrying.

Thomas returned, and she sent him to the smokehouse for the ham she'd selected the day before. Milly and Loven would be missing it, but they had meat put up as well—and this was too important.

Making sure everyone else was dressed for the trek up the mountain, Truth put on her hunting coat and strapped both hers and Papa's shot pouches and powder horns across her body. Lastly, she returned to the back room for the bundle she'd prepared the night before. Once that was slung in place, she put on her hat, took both her rifle and Papa's in hand, and led off into the snowy morning.

"Where are we going?" Mercy asked.

"I bet it has something to do with Micah," Thomas said.

"Silly, we're taking Christmas to him," Patience said.

Truth smiled a little. Her sister was as sharp as any.

"Are you going to marry him, Truth?" Thankful asked.

"We saw him kiss you," Thomas said.

"How could you not," Truth muttered, but she smiled wider.

Micah, unashamed, kissing her in the front yard for God and everyone to see.

"Are you going to marry him?" Patience asked.

She laughed. "I just might."

Thomas and the younger girls broke out into whoops and huzzahs.

"Wait," Mercy said. "Is he still a Tory?"

Truth laughed until she was breathless—which wasn't long, considering they'd hit a steep portion of the trail.

~*~*~*~

Micah had always loved snow. On this morning, he stepped out of the cave and was struck breathless by the clear glory surrounding him.

As pure as the first Christmas morning, he was sure.

Filling his lungs with the crisp, clean-washed mountain air, he scanned the forest. Did he risk leaving tracks for a quick run to the lookout at the summit?

Aye, how could he not?

The chill air burned his nostrils and invigorated as he raced up the now-well-known track. Glimpses of the snow-covered distance flashed between the trees, white and shadow stark in the dawn, but he pressed on until he came to the familiar tumble of boulders.

At the top, he feasted his eyes. First toward the east, and away southward in the misty distance, past the rippled mountaintops, the land that had birthed and bred him. He thought of his parents, gone these many years, and of the bitter struggle between John and Zacharias during the early part of the war, before Zach had gone to join the Continentals. His sisters, busying themselves in their growing families, and only speaking of Zach in whispers, after.

His own idealistic fervor until the awfulness that was Kings Mountain.

The world did not hold enough treasure to tempt him to trade places with the rebels, not with the way their officers had left the fallen prisoners to be trampled to death on the march by day, and then vented their fury upon them by night. But after watching the settlements scratching for survival here on the frontier, and furthermore, living it as he'd sought to help Truth, his heart had changed. He was no stranger to hardship, being backcountry folk himself, but their raw determination amazed him.

He turned slowly, his gaze marking where hillside fell away into river valley. Could he indeed find his place here, if Truth made the decision to accept him?

And if she did not, where would he go? Possibly home, to see his sisters a last time, at least. But after, then what?

Heart aching, he searched the edge of the valley, where he knew Truth's farm lay past the folds of the mountainsides. *Oh God, can she forgive who I am ... who I was?*

Then there was the matter of how long she might wait to let him know what she'd decided. Would she make him stay here the whole winter long, hoping he'd simply leave?

He blew out a long breath, watching the plume of steam disappear on the breeze. Enough already. Christmas day or no, he had snares to check. At the least, he'd have a bundle of furs to carry down to the fort and trade in a few weeks. The keeper of the post had promised whatever provisions he wished in exchange. It was just rabbit and squirrel now, but if he could barter or work for a decent rifle, there was more to be made in deer or bear pelts.

The longing hit him like a blow to the chest, and he shut his eyes. *Oh Truth ...*

A shot echoed across the mountainside, and he

looked up again, scanning the forest. An odd morning for someone to be out hunting, and this community didn't seem to be given to the customary *feu de joi* of the lower country. But no more shots followed, and after a few minutes of listening, Micah climbed down off the rocks and went to check his snares.

They'd passed Truth's favorite hunting rock, and as they neared the cave where she'd found Micah taking shelter all those weeks ago, she found her heart beating unaccountably fast.

You know where to find me. Would he even be there?

Ah Lord, let him be there!

They rounded the last bend, and she made everyone stop at the big oak where she'd stood signaling for him that first time. She handed the rifles off to Patience, then facing the half-hidden cave entrance, pursed her lips and sent out the call again. *Whippoorwill! Whippoorwill!*

Silence, and the wind in the bare treetops above, rattling the few browned leaves remaining.

Her heart plummeted. What if he'd gone away already?

Then her eye caught on the fresh prints laid in the snow, leading from the cave entrance. Her pulse leaped anew.

"Here—hold my rifle and stay here until I tell you otherwise," she said, taking Papa's rifle from Patience.

She wouldn't go far—surely he'd be back, and they had plenty of preparations to make before their feast would be ready. But she couldn't resist tracking him a short distance, at least.

Cradling the rifle, she set off up the trail. She recognized the winding path—so he'd gone to the lookout? It had been a while since she'd been there herself—

And then—there he was, climbing toward her from a slightly different path, winding upward through the laurel. He stopped, eyes widening, then hurried on toward her. A pair of rabbits dangled from his hand.

She could hardly breathe, of a sudden.

He stopped a few paces from her, head angled, eyes searching her face. His chest rose and fell—the climb, or her sudden appearance? Warmth shivered through her at the thought that she might affect him as much as he did her. She certainly couldn't seem to find her tongue.

"Truth," he breathed.

Of habit, she glanced over his gear—haversack, knife, hat, gaiters, mittens. "You're missing a few things there," she blurted.

The corner of his mouth tipped. "I've been doing all right."

"Well—" She forced her feet to move forward a step. "You need—this."

And she held out Papa's rifle.

A flush crossed his pale cheek. He searched her eyes, then hesitantly reached for it. "You're—certain?"

She nodded, sure her own cheeks must be red as

holly berries. They felt hot enough to catch on fire.

He gently, reverently, took the piece from her hands. Her throat closed, and she unstrapped Papa's powder horn and shot bag. "These too," she whispered.

He took them, looped them one-handed across shoulders and over his body. "Figured you'd be saving them for Thomas," he murmured.

She shook her head, swallowing. "It's my thought … they won't be leaving the family."

He went still, and she could not tear herself away from the hope in his dark eyes.

"If what you said to me last time means what I think it does," she went on.

A smile dawned, flashed into a grin. "Sweet Truth. This is your answer?"

Oh, he made her both soft and weak. She could only manage another nod. What if she'd mistaken his intent?

He eased closer, knuckles brushing her cheek. His brows knitted for a moment. "You'd forgive me enough to marry me?"

Another nod. She was drowning in those eyes.

He took off his hat, swept an arm around her, and kissed her with such suddenness that her own hat fell off. But she only kissed him back, reveling in the contrast of warm lips and cold cheekbone, and in the strength of him in her arms.

After a very long moment—or several—he pulled back, breathless. "Surely you didn't come alone?"

She giggled. "No. I left the young'uns at the cave. We brought Christmas dinner."

~*~*~*~

Micah could hardly believe the happy blur of the next hours. Tramping hand in hand back to the cave, where Thomas and all three girls jumped for joy and cheered, then flew toward him with open arms. They'd brought not only a ham but a turkey—that was the shot he'd heard from the lookout—and half of them set to dressing the bird while the other half stoked the fire inside the cave and set up the spit. The pumpkins were tucked around the edges of the fire for roasting, and when all was set for the long wait of cooking, Truth sat them down and laid the Bible in his lap. "Would you do us the honor of reading?"

He met her pleading half smile with a grin of his own, then opened to where she'd already marked the passage with a scrap of ribbon. The print read, *The Gospel According to Luke,* and she pointed to chapter two.

This task had always been taken by his father, and then by his eldest brother. It wasn't that he disbelieved, but Micah had felt detached from the words they'd read—pronouncements and decrees from an ancient, distant God. But today, touching the pages and seeing the expectant faces surrounding him, as the firelight flickered on the cave walls, Micah thought he sensed the nearness of God as never before.

Had God truly heard and answered his prayers?

Truth leaned toward him, her fingers covering his on the page. "We had our reading last night, for

Christmas Eve. But this—this is why we came today." Her eyes, pale as mist, begged him to understand. "Just—read it, and I'll explain."

With a nod, he found his place and began. "And it came to pass in those days, that a decree went out from Caesar Augustus, that all the world should be taxed ….

"...For mine eyes have seen thy salvation, which thou hast prepared before the face of all people; a light to lighten the Gentiles, and the glory of thy people Israel."

Truth's hand covered his again, and he looked up.

"This is why," she said, her voice soft, her gaze earnest. "On Christmas we celebrate the birth of the Christ, yes? The One that God sent to later die for our sins. Mine, Micah, as well as yours."

"And what sins might you have, sweet Truth?" He knew well his own.

"Pride," she answered, without hesitation. "But—His grace covers it all. And I cannot expect Him to forgive me if I'm not willing to forgive you.

"Whether or not you were directly responsible for Papa's death—" She faltered, and blinked. "You did not know, and it's past. You are here now. And I'd be wrong to refuse this gift of grace that God is offering me, in you."

He turned his hand to clasp hers, and she gripped it tightly. Those misty eyes shimmered in the firelight.

For a moment he nearly forgot they were not alone.

"And I confess I've become—" he was sure she

blushed— "accustomed to having you about."

A chorus of giggles greeted that pronouncement. With a grin, he took them all in. "And what are your thoughts about this?"

Patience only smiled shyly, but Thomas snorted and said, "You'd better marry her while you can. She's never let anyone else get close enough to kiss her."

And while they all laughed—Micah and Truth included—Micah set aside the Bible, rose to his feet, and drew Truth into his arms. She nestled into his embrace, then tipped her head so her mouth was close to his ear. "Of a certain, you're the only one I'd want defending me," she whispered.

Warmed through, and not by the fire, he tucked her closer. "For the rest of my life," he murmured back.

Author's Note

Truth and her papa and siblings are fictional, but I've anchored them within an actual historical family. Anthony Bledsoe was indeed captain of the home guard while the others rode away to hunt Ferguson, and genealogical records reveal a much younger half brother by the whimsical name of Loving Bledsoe—by some accounts, Lovin or Loven. Where I could, I matched family members as well as events with historical records. Although I kept their location deliberately vague, they probably lived in or around the Watauga Valley in what is now eastern Tennessee, but was then western North Carolina.

In reality, Truth's younger brother would have been considered old enough to run the hills and go hunting for the family, so that was a bit of dramatic license on my part. (Although it might not be farfetched if someone in the family expressed a bad feeling about letting him roam and wander, considering what his future held!) I did not, however, exaggerate the tales told after the terrible battle at Kings Mountain, which was a major turning point in America's war for independence.

My apologies to the descendants of Joseph Greer, for painting that bold and daring young man in a less than flattering light.

For those who may not have read it yet, Thomas has

his own story in the volume *The Cumberland Bride,* a 2018 release from Barbour Publishing and #5 of the Daughters of the Mayflower.

The Counterfeit Tory

The text of this story previously appeared in *The Backcountry Brides Collection* by Barbour Publishing. It has since been modified and updated.

For Don Mallicoat—
the man I called Daddy, who showed me
what honorable manhood looks like.
Thank you for having
a heart to protect the wounded.
I still miss you.

And for Mom—
who first saw something worth encouraging
in my writing. Though I bitterly miss you, too,
I'm so glad you and Daddy
are beholding the face of Jesus together.

Acknowledgements

(new to the 2023 edition)

I owe so much to so many people…

My dear writing friends and critique partners Lee, Ronie, Beth, Jen, and Michelle, who over the years have listened, empathized, prayed, and sometimes preached…and challenged me to be the best writer I can be.

Editor Becky Germany and agent Tamela Hancock Murray for believing in my stories, and for Ellen Tarver for her sharp eye on the details.

Author and Revolutionary War reenactor Patrick O'Kelley for his painstaking research on every military action in the Carolinas during the American Revolution. Without his work, I'd never feel confident tackling this era.

Other friends and extended family who ask every so often, "How is your writing coming?" with genuine interest, even or maybe especially through the dry spells. Your kindness has been the rain that kept hope alive.

My husband Troy, who has always believed in me, even when it meant sending me to conference year after year with no apparent return, and my darling children—that includes you, the spouses!—who have been amazingly supportive and enthusiastic, even when my dedication to writing looked like neglect on your side. I tell you again, I would not be who I am without you!

And lastly, but most importantly, to our Lord and Savior, Creator of the universe, the original Storyteller Himself. Any glory here is His.

Prologue

Charlotte Town, North Carolina, mid-November 1781

"Do these people even know they've lost the war?"

"Obviously not."

Tucked in a corner of the tavern where the babble of conversation was not quite louder than his own thoughts, Jedidiah Wheeler dropped the much-folded paper on the tabletop and stared at it with distaste. "And why can't we leave this rascal to Sumter and Marion?"

Harrison leaned on one elbow, dark gaze intent. "We need someone on the inside. Someone he doesn't know yet. Someone he could possibly trust. Doesn't have to be for long."

Jed chewed the inside of his cheek, thinking. "A man would have to have a death wish to accept this appointment."

A smirk twisted the other man's mouth. "I've heard of your exploits over the past five years. One could say that description fits you."

'Twas true he'd little enough to lose. An occupation that became useless with the tide of war sweeping the colonies for the past five years and more. A mother and then a father who succumbed to age and illness during that time.

A sweetheart who spurned him for another,

despite her avowed admiration for his service in the militia. And fine by him. He'd always welcomed the adventure that went along with riding first with the local militia and later with the Continental Regulars.

"I'd like to live long enough to return to riding the Great Road up to Philly," he groused.

This time Harrison laughed outright. "Now you're just being sentimental. Deadly dull, that."

Jed lifted his fingers dismissively.

"Besides," Harrison went on, "no one lives forever. And this rapscallion and his band must be stopped. Could you sleep at night if you didn't at least make the attempt?"

"Mm. Next you'll be singing about king and country."

Harrison gave a silent laugh that disappeared under a wave of uncharacteristic sternness. "Outright slaughter, Jed. And after they'd surrendered. For the sake of all that's true and holy."

The weight of it pressed upon his chest. "One could say that about either side." He'd seen enough of the brutality Whigs and Tories meted upon each other these last several years. And gotten his fill of it.

But the fact that weeks after the surrender of Cornwallis at Yorktown, loyalists still rampaged across the Carolina countryside, stuck in his craw as much as it did Harrison's. He'd just not admit it, yet.

The severity of the other man's expression did not ease. Jed heaved a great sigh—not entirely manufactured—and slapped a hand across the letter. "Very well."

One might as well die doing something honorable as not.

Chapter 1

Ninety Six District, the South Carolina backcountry, November 1781

"Lizzy! Where is my good waistcoat?"

Leaning on her broom, Lizzy Cunningham suppressed a huff. "Hanging where you left it, I expect," she called back, then muttered, "Such a shock that you can't find a wife, Dickie."

With firm strokes, she continued sweeping behind the tavern counter. Why would her brothers seek wives when they had a ready servant in their sister?

"Now, don't be like that, Lizzy girl," her father boomed as he rounded the doorjamb, leaning heavily on his cane. "Your brother works hard and deserves a little help."

Schooling her expression, she tucked her head and kept at the task. He couldn't hear her thoughts. Truly.

"A little help don't mean he can't find his own clothing." The words were out before she could stop them.

Papa lumbered toward her, thunder in his face and step, despite the limp. Lizzy gripped the broom and steeled herself—running would only cause him to be harsher later—but he glanced past her and halted, rearranging his face into the false pleasantry she hated.

"Hullo! What can we do for you this fine day?"

"Something hot to drink would be welcome," came a smooth, low voice behind her.

Lizzy returned to her sweeping.

"We've mulled cider, or did you wish something stronger?" Papa shuffled past her with a hard pinch to her upper arm, under the guise of affection.

"Cider is fine. Too early for a toddy."

She couldn't place the voice, but that meant naught. And she wouldn't turn to see, and draw more attention to herself—

"Lizzy, look sharp," Papa said. "Get the man a cider."

With the slightest of curtsies, she scurried to lean the broom against the wall, then fetched an earthenware tankard and went to the hearth to fill it from the kettle hanging there.

She slid it across the counter with practiced swiftness, aiming for the man's open grasp without looking up into his face. Best to keep her head down, not invite any more attention than need be. But when his other hand reached up to remove a dusty cocked hat trimmed in braid and black ribbon—a fancy sort, given the worn hunting shirt and rifleman's gear—her curiosity betrayed her with a flicked glance upward. His face was a broad, honest one, the kind a body would instinctively trust and forget, after. Blue eyes met hers directly, then crinkled into a smile.

Warmth flooded her. She let go of the tankard and whirled away.

~*~*~*~

Gracious, but the girl was skittish.

Jed wanted to watch her, see if he could catch her attention again, even for a moment, but his focus was commanded by the man he presumed to be proprietor, leaning on his cane. Who, if Jed did not miss his guess, had been about to strike the girl.

Not his concern, he supposed, but—the thought brought a burn to the back of his throat.

The man shifted his bulk closer, his expression wheedling. "Have you business here?"

"I do," Jed said, slowly, deliberately sipping the cider. Not bad. He glanced around the near-empty common room. Clean enough, if shabby. Provisions looked sparse, but the war had been unkind to all, regardless of partisan leanings. "Name's Jed Williams." He offered his hand.

The older man shifted, and after the merest hesitation, shook the outstretched hand. "Charles Cunningham." He twitched a nod toward the girl. "My daughter. My two boys are elsewhere, working."

Jed kept his smile amiable. "A fine establishment you have here." It had nothing on many of the taverns and ordinaries he'd frequented on the Great Road north, but…the war had been hard on everyone.

His flattery had its intended effect, however. Cunningham drew himself up. "We do well enough."

"Indeed. P'raps you can help me with a delicate matter."

The older man's gaze sharpened with interest.

"I seek a man. Told you are a relative of his—as are others in these parts, but that you are trustworthy."

If he kept this up, he'd need to spend half the night in prayer, repenting of falsehoods.

"Aye?"

"A certain Captain Cunningham—William, I believe?"

"Aye. That's my nephew Billy. A major now, he is. The British gave him a promotion for his service to the Crown."

"Ah, good to hear." Jed let his grin melt into the semblance of a worried frown. "I'd like to speak with this Captain—I mean, Major—Cunningham. Ask if I might join him. Cast out of my own home by these blasted rebels, myself."

The tavern proprietor's brow creased. "Well, now. That might be tricky. A body never knows when Billy might show up. Or where he might be next. But if you were to stick around, like—I might be able to find something out for you. We have a room available for let, as well."

Jed clapped a companionable hand on the older man's shoulder. "Many thanks, my good man. I'd be right obliged."

Cunningham's head bobbed. His smile grew more greasy, if such a thing were possible. "Now then, I must go see to matters. I'll return shortly. Might we provide you something to eat?"

"I'd be grateful for that as well."

Jed watched him circle through the common room so he could nudge the girl still busy at her task of sweeping and mutter something to her. She cast Jed a glance, gave her father a stiff nod, and followed him back to the rear of the tavern.

He released a long sigh and turned to give the place a better look. Again, clean enough, if shabby, but something about it made his skin crawl to think of staying here overnight. *God in heaven, protect me.*

Not the first time he'd uttered those words. Wouldn't be the last, either, he was sure.

Chapter 2

Lizzy stirred down the stew and reached for a wooden bowl. Just outside the kitchen, Papa had summoned Dickie, who apparently managed to locate his own waistcoat after all. "Take the horse and find your cousin. Let him know there's a man here what wants to speak with him. Appears to be alone, at that."

Her cousin could not be too careful about who joined him or even professed interest in such, she knew. Not that it mattered one whit to her what kind of trouble he found himself in. The district had been markedly quieter while Billy stayed in exile in Florida those two years. Billy couldn't resist causing a stir wherever he went.

And this stray fellow wanting to come join Billy's regiment? Must be either a simpleton or fellow mischief maker.

She slid a roll from a larger, covered bowl on the counter into the stew, hesitated, then grabbed a second. Papa would chide her generosity—possibly—but the bread needed eaten. And she was sick of seeing Papa and her brothers gobble it all down before anyone else got to enjoy it.

Back to the common room, then, while Papa and Dickie continued whispering together. Still standing at the counter, the stranger turned at her entrance. There went that smile again, meant to be charming, she was sure. They always tried to be charming, at least until they'd had a taste of her scalding tongue. Papa scolded her for it, but if he wished her to be biddable to every clod who walked through that door—

"I expect you'll want to sit down," she said, angling for one of the side tables. "Does this suit you?"

The smile didn't waver. If anything, it brightened, making his unremarkable face something she'd want to stop and study, under other circumstances. The blue eyes twinkled as his head dipped. "Suits fine, thank you."

Simpleton, then. She felt a stab of pity for the life that awaited him with her cousin's regiment.

After setting down the bowl and spoon, she sidled away to retrieve her broom.

"So, your cousin," came the man's voice, catching her halfway across the room. "He's a fair man to ride with, by all accounts?"

She plucked the broom from where it stood against the wall and turned to face him. "'Tain't from around here, are you?"

His expression maintained a steady pleasantry as he shoveled in a bite of stew, those eyes still sparkling as if they shared a secret between them. But he didn't reply.

"Well." She applied herself to the last bit of floor she'd already covered. "Some say he's fair enough. Some say he's a right terror."

He nodded thoughtfully, scooped a second bite. "Word has it he first enlisted with the rebel side, when all your family are good royalists."

Lizzy couldn't help her derisive snort. "Wouldn't necessarily call us 'good' royalists. Not all of us." He chewed steadily, still watching her, so she swept with more attention, but the words continued creeping out of her. "He always had a terrible need to make his own way. Have his own opinions. I'm sure 'twas to spite his daddy if nothing else, at least at first. Then when he discovered it meant he'd have to follow orders and go where he didn't always want to…"

Why did this man's gaze make her feel so squirmy inside, and yet comfortable talking, at the same time?

"So he was court martialed for insubordination and flogged," he said, then lifted the spoon toward her in salute. "This is right toothsome. You make it?"

She likewise couldn't stop the flush of pleasure that swept over her. She muted her response to a short nod.

She wasn't adding that her father's own loyalties could be wobbly, at best. But Jed couldn't fault her for leaving out that detail, not to someone who purported to be enough of a hotheaded loyalist himself to join Bill Cunningham.

The girl was a contradiction. Quiet industry yet ill at ease. Reluctant to speak even while she spilled bits of information, sweeping that floor as if her life depended on it.

Perhaps it did.

He forced himself to eat slowly, remembering all the times rations were thin while on campaign. And making the stew last longer gave him more time for observation.

The tavern keeper hadn't yet reappeared, which surprised him. His gaze strayed back to the girl. Thin, stoop-shouldered, clad in a petticoat so faded he could barely tell it had once been blue, and a plain brown gown that pinched at the elbows and barely lapped across her front. The tavern keeper couldn't spare a coin to dress his own daughter decently?

But then, the war had been hard on all…

She wore no cap, either—not that he cared about that. Many girls across the backcountry dispensed with such niceties, but she carried herself with such a proper air, it surprised him. Her hair fell braided, straight down her back, of a shade just darker than the gown.

What color were her eyes?

As if she'd heard his thought, she glanced toward him, affording him a glimpse of her pale, severe face, then twitched away again, head tucked even lower than before.

And what hurts had she suffered to make her so mistrustful? Fire swept his veins at the thought.

"Miss Cunningham—"

Her father chose that moment to lumber through the door. His gaze darted to the girl and back to Jed before a forced smile creased his face again. "'Tis all set. My son will ride to inform my nephew of your presence here, and Lizzy will have your room prepared. The horse out front is yours?"

"Aye. I'll see to her stabling, save you the trouble."

The man seemed to relax a mite. "Shed's out back, with fodder. Just come in the back entrance when you're done."

Jed rose, dipped his head to Miss Cunningham, who hesitated but didn't quite acknowledge him—watching him without looking at him directly—and gathered his hat and rifle.

He found the shed in an arguably better state than the common room, as far as repair and outfitting. Jed smiled grimly as he tied his bay mare into an open stall. Wouldn't be the first time men demanded better accommodations for their horses than for themselves. In fact, if the situation were any less precarious, he'd be tempted to bunk out here with Daisy rather than inside the tavern.

Not that as a tavern, they were as used to hosting overnight guests. The place was supposed to serve as a social center for a town or, in this case, a stopping point for travelers between towns, but the apparent dearth of actual social activity bespoke…what? What could he gather from this situation?

After removing the saddle and setting it over the side of the stall, Jed took a bunch of hay and commenced to rubbing Daisy down.

With the recent push by the Continental army under General Greene to clear all loyalists from the backcountry, apparently this tavern keeper, known by many to have loyalist leanings, found it hard to continue doing business among his patriot neighbors. *Rebel,* he reminded himself. If he were to pass himself off as one of these men, he needed to keep the proper verbiage firmly in mind. A proper Tory did not think of his Whig neighbors as anything but the sorest of revolutionaries. Even in the face of obvious defeat.

He vented a sigh. Could he even carry this off?

Chapter 3

The common room had been swept and tables wiped down for the night—not that they'd seen many customers this eve—and the kitchen tidied and prepared for the morrow. Perhaps she could get to bed now.

She climbed the stairs, weary to her bones, as she so often was at the close of a day. Down the hall, almost tiptoeing so as not to rouse her father and brothers and give them a reason to task her with one more thing. Or a dozen.

So intent was she on remaining silent that when the door to the lone guest room swung open and its occupant stepped out, he was as startled by her presence as she by his. But he recovered quickly and flashed a grin. "Good eve, Miss—"

She put a finger to her lips, and he fell obligingly silent.

Not a complete simpleton, perhaps.

The grin faded, his gaze sharpening. A scrape sounded inside Robert's room, and his door creaked open. "Lizzy! I need you to—"

Beside her, their overnight guest straightened and said, "Pardon. I have need of Miss Cunningham at the moment. Might it wait?"

Her brother's expression went sly. "You do, do you? Well, now." His eyes slid toward her. "I suppose, then…what I need…can wait."

And with great hesitation and obvious reluctance, he withdrew.

Heart pounding but trying not to show it, Lizzy turned back to—"Mr. Williams, is it?"

Something flickered in the man's eyes. "Aye." The smile resurfaced, but with reserve. "Miss Cunningham. My apologies."

"Mine as well," she said, suddenly breathless under his gaze, and made to dodge past him.

He caught her by the shoulder, light but firm. She flinched, and he released her immediately.

"Miss Cunningham—"

"Please," she whispered. "Not here." Meeting his look fully for the first time, she glanced meaningfully toward her brother's door and back.

He nodded slowly, stepping back. "Where, then?" he mouthed.

She shook her head and edged along the wall. His hand came up and stopped.

"I wish you no hurt, Miss Cunningham," he murmured.

She stared at his hand, which turned, palm up. The arm remained outstretched, his face, grave.

Then she did the only thing that made any sense—turned and fled down the hallway and up the narrow set of stairs leading to her attic room. Once inside, she barred the door, as she had every night since she was a young girl, and stood panting against it.

Did such a man exist, who wished her no hurt?

~*~*~*~

Jed stood, still reeling with disbelief. What on earth had this girl suffered, that she'd not even stop to speak with him?

He lingered until the sound of her footfalls ended with the close of the door, then crept down the hall in the opposite direction. His contact would wait, but Jed didn't want to delay any more than needed.

Downstairs, out through the tavern's back door, he angled toward the necessary, glancing all around without seeming to, stopping between the necessary and stable to listen. Then he pressed on, into the thickets.

He found the great, multi-trunked maple with little trouble, climbed into the middle, and released a soft whippoorwill call. A similar call answered, then with a rustle, a shadowy form emerged from along the creek. "Jedidiah Wheeler?"

"Williams for now." Jed stepped back into view. "And you are…?" He knew better than to speak a name first.

"Zacharias Elliot." The man offered his hand, and Jed shook it with good will. "Pleased to make your acquaintance. Even more pleased that you took this task…though I do not envy you the carrying of it out."

Jed gave a low laugh. "Nay. 'Tis not to be envied, for sure. I've been lodged for the night and hope to meet the man himself on the morrow or the next day, but the whole place smells of something gone very amiss."

The other man folded his arms across his chest. "You mean, more than them being Tory?" When Jed hesitated, he snorted softly. "Fear not to speak.

My own family were staunch loyalists. They turned me out when I turned coat."

"Speaking of an unenviable position," Jed said, with respect.

Elliot's head dipped.

"And aye," he went on, slowly, "of something more than that."

'Twas on the tip of his tongue to say something about the girl, but that was not useful intelligence of any sort.

At least not yet. Jed could not shake the niggle that he needed to keep an eye on her.

"I've no idea how often I'll be able to report," he said.

"Understandably. Is there someone at the tavern I might entrust messages to?"

"I'd say avoid the tavern keeper and his boys. But the daughter seems to be a solid enough sort."

Elliot's head came up a little. "Could she be recruited, do you think?"

Jed shrugged. But he couldn't say the idea hadn't occurred to him. "I'll see what I can do."

Chapter 4

When Jed returned to the tavern, a contingent of mounted riders roughly circled the building.

He drew a long breath then emerged from the thicket, straightening his clothing as if returning from nothing more than a leisurely trip to the necessary. Several men swung toward him, weapons raised. About half wore frontier or farmer's garb, the other half regimentals. Green ones, if he didn't misgauge it in the gloom, typical of loyalist troops. "Good evening, gentlemen. What might I help you with?"

"Are you Williams?" one of the regimentals asked.

"I am."

The plumed hat tipped toward the tavern. "Come with us."

Feeling as though he already had a knife stuck in his gut, Jed went along.

Inside, the common room was lit again by a pair of candelabras, where half a dozen men sat at table and a dozen more lined the walls. The color of the regimentals was a definite green, as he'd guessed. Miss Cunningham scurried along the edges of the group, pitcher in hand, filling tankards as they were lifted. He suppressed a wince at the hunch of her shoulders and gave his attention to the men.

And all their attention was on him. This must be

what Daniel felt, being tossed into the lions' den.

He stepped to the middle of the common room and slowly looked around, hands loose at his sides, letting them gauge him as he did them. A motley bunch they were, but no more rough looking than the Continentals and militia he'd ridden with these past months.

The war had been hard on them all…

Dismissing the thought, he scanned their faces and met the eyes of each one in the half light. Ordinary felt hats with pine sprigs shaded lean faces, most clean shaven but some with a few days of whiskers. Several Indians as well, bright bits of color against their shirts and leggings, regarding him impassively.

No one moved. They barely breathed. At last, one man in regimentals rose from his seat nearby, unfolding to his full height, easily a hand or so taller than Jed. "I'm Major William Cunningham. You wished to meet with me?"

A well-formed man, he was, and young, no older than Jed himself. Yet commanding. All the other men watched him like trained hounds.

"I did." The trick here would be to strike the right balance of adulation and comradeship. A man like this thrived under having his pride stoked. "Heard you're one of the best to ride with if a man wants to strike back at these blasted rebels."

Cunningham shifted, and his eyes glittered. "And striking back would be your desire, would it?"

"Aye," Jed answered, without hesitation. "Turned out of my home, I was. And with them rascals overrunning the whole of the Carolinas—"

"Where was your home?" Cunningham smoothly interposed.

"North Carolina. Mecklenburg County." Exchanged glances and nods all around at that. "My parents are dead, God rest their souls. No other family willing to have me." He swallowed. That part wasn't strictly true, but he mustn't give it away. Although a little emotion could go a long way toward convincing the others.

"And what mischief were you at, outside?"

"Mischief?" Jed blinked. "Weren't nothing but a trip to the necessary. Except someone were in there, so I—ah—" He slanted a glance at Miss Cunningham.

William Cunningham turned to his female cousin. "Lizzy?"

Jed's heart thudded painfully in his chest. This small thing could be his undoing—

The girl straightened, facing them. Color washed faintly across her cheeks. "Aye, I'd gone out. What of it?"

Air filled his lungs, but Jed barely caught himself from gaping.

Why would she cover for him?

Whatever had possessed her to do that?

Lizzy could see the slight widening of his eyes—the recognition that she knew he was being untruthful there somewhere—but for some reason, maybe the hopeless wish that he truly was as kind as he seemed, she couldn't resist defying her cousin for his sake.

Said cousin released a humorless chuckle as she turned away. "Surely he hasn't been here long enough to secure your affections already, Lizzy?"

"What matter is it to you?" she threw back over her shoulder. "As you all so often remind me, not a man's been made who could bear living with me."

The room exploded with laughter. All except for Mr. Williams, who regarded her with a look of puzzlement and—was that distress? Or merely pity?

She turned her back on him as well. She knew she wasn't well favored. Why heap hurt upon hurt by pretending she ever had the slightest chance to catch his eye?

Not that she wanted to. He was a man, like any other, who only wanted a woman for keeping his house and bearing his children. And she'd not met one yet that she'd willingly shackle herself to, much less risk childbed for.

This one was cool as you please, however. Her cousin was a cruel, bloody man—she did not doubt the accounts that floated back over the past weeks, not when he was wont to come in and brag on his exploits. This stranger had to know that. And yet he answered Billy's questions and cross-questions with no hesitation.

It almost disappointed her to think he'd go riding with Billy without even a show of caution. But—if he was the simpleton she'd first thought him, or worse, he'd bear the penalty for it. And rightfully so. No business was it of hers if he brought perdition down on his own head.

Suddenly weary beyond bearing, she returned to

the kitchen on the pretext of fetching something, and listened as Billy pronounced the stranger, Jed Williams, fit to join his company.

No business of hers at all.

Chapter 5

Survival was easy the first day.

As a new rider in the company, Jed was expected to do little more than keep up and stand watch. He felt the probing gazes of Cunningham and the others, but as long as he kept quiet, eyes open, laughed along at their jesting, and nodded sagely at their ranting, he invited no undue attention and thus, no trouble.

Such good fortune couldn't last forever.

Around the fire that first night—they'd camped at Cunningham's Tavern and taken provisions the next morning before being on their way—he listened to the men's talk, making note of names and where they were from, asking his own questions when he could about why they were there. A common thread of pride bound them all. The overall cause was not so much striking back at a rebellion that had managed to bring the best troops of Mother England to their knees just weeks before, but how that rebellion had hurt them all in personal ways. One man's wife had been accidentally shot and killed through the door by her own brother during one of the many skirmishes flaring across the Carolinas over the past couple of years. Though both men grieved hard, in the end neither could be reconciled to the other's views.

Many told tales similar to Bill Cunningham's, of

family members abused by rebel neighbors, crops and livestock ruined or taken, homes burned or confiscated. What had any of them left, besides carrying out as much retribution as possible against those who smugly remained? None wanted to sit in Charles Town and merely wait for transportation elsewhere.

Jed did not doubt the truth of any of their stories. If anything, he'd guess they were more sparing in detail than they could have been. Just weeks ago he'd left the company of Rutherford, who had exercised such severity against loyalists, regardless of sex or age, that General Greene himself warned him to back off, or he'd authorize the loyalists to retaliate.

One or two of the men here mentioned Rutherford. Jed suppressed a sigh. Sitting here, his face warmed by a fire while the November evening cooled his back, surrounded by anger and sorrow and desperation, he could almost be in sympathy with these men.

Not that he entirely blamed Rutherford, either. The man had spent some months in a prison ship in Charles Town harbor.

A very dangerous position he found himself in, but perhaps he could make it serve.

He lifted his head. "So what of the events at Turner's Station?"

They stared at him as if he were an imbecile. He felt rather like one, but it needed to be asked.

"You must understand," one of the men said at last. He cast a glance over his shoulder at another fire several dozen paces away, where Cunningham himself lounged with those Jed had learned already were his most-trusted officers, then lowered his voice. "Our wives and children have been thrown out of their homes and forced to the road as refugees—many times with nary a possession but the clothes on their backs. What man of honor does that? And what sort of men would we be if we didn't answer such cruelty on their behalf?"

Jed offered a slow nod.

"See then, the major has determined to hunt down the rascals responsible for these and other despicable acts. Only he knows the full list, or in what order he plans to attack."

"Turner's Station was just one of several," another man said. "Those what died, deserved it. Although"—and Jed could see the man shudder as he looked away—"none of us would argue that the major wasn't a little mad with bloodshed. 'Tis one thing to shoot or hang a man for his crimes, another thing entirely to hew him in pieces."

What a perfect nightmare he'd been dropped into.

Lizzy hated nights like this one. Full already, and then her cousin's men stopped in for refreshment. If only she could hide in her attic room. Or at least the kitchen. But Papa always insisted she be on hand to serve.

Hooting laughter erupted from a dice game in the corner. Suppressing a wince, she deposited the platter of sliced bread and apples on the counter and made to turn away when their overnight guest from several days ago leaned toward her and caught her gaze. "Quite the crowd this evening, Miss Cunningham."

She glanced across the room, taking in not only the games that were yet just short of unruly, and her father holding court near the hearth—it could be called nothing else—and gave a short nod. "Fair enough, it is."

He chuckled, leaning his elbow on the counter. "Come now. A bit more than fair, I'd call it."

With a long, cool look, she straightened and turned, but his hand brushed her sleeve. She yanked away and gave him as scorching a glare as she could summon. His suddenly grave, earnest gaze caught her, however, as his physical touch could not.

"My apologies, Miss Cunningham. Have you been—well?"

"Well enough." Somehow the sharp retort on her lips lost the edge she'd intended.

His eyes searched hers. "What qualifies as 'well enough,' I wonder."

A hot ache bloomed in her chest. "Do not toy with me, Mr. Williams. I am no simpering doxy to be taken in by your sweet words."

Surprise flashed across his expression, then he broke out in another laugh. "Nay. You are most certainly not that."

And as he laughed again—yet not in a way that seemed to be at her expense—the hurt melted and a slight smile tugged at her mouth. She ducked her head lest he see it and misread it as friendliness.

Too late. His hand extended across the counter again. "Please. I only meant to ask—were there any messages for me?"

She slid away. "Nay. No messages."

She scurried back to the kitchen, and pressed the heel of her hand to the middle of her chest, over the worn stiffening of her stays. What was it about him?

And why was he asking about messages?

Chapter 6

"Not much call for a rifle in the work of retribution," Kittery commented. "But that's a right fine pair of dragoon pistols."

Jed hardly glanced at the fine Pennsylvania long rifle hanging from his saddle, tucked snugly under his knee. "It goes where I go," he said mildly. "Where are we headed this misty morning?"

Kittery snickered. "Meet up with Hezekiah Williams, below Ninety Six. Any relation of yours?"

Jed pretended to think, then shook his head.

He'd joined up, he already knew, at the end of a three-day spree—executions, Cunningham called them—of noted Whig leaders across the South Carolina backcountry.

Cunningham's list wasn't near exhausted yet.

Please, Lord, help me to stay true. Help me to do what's right. Help me put an end to this, and if I share in the bloodguilt in any way... I beg your forgiveness.

He thought of Lizzy, serving so faithfully back at her father's tavern. The startled look on her face when he'd asked after her welfare. How in that one moment she'd let him get close enough, he could see flecks of blue and green and gold in her dark eyes—all the colors of a Carolina autumn day.

The shock that had gone through him when she'd

actually smiled—just a little, but a definite smile nevertheless, one that had banished the pale severity and transformed her.

Lord, protect her. And let me live to get back and make her smile again. That girl needs more reasons to smile.

But mostly, protect her.

Another morning, another day to get through.

And to make things worse, while she scrubbed the tavern floor, on her knees, the memory of blue eyes and an earnest-sounding inquiry lingering at the edges of her thoughts.

This was why she locked her heart up tight and refused to entertain silly notions, such as the hope that a man could be honorable and good. Such hints either turned out to cover dark motives, or they came from someone who wouldn't stay once they saw the ugliness of her own heart. And in the meantime she was left longing for something she could never have.

Maybe 'twas time to do as other women did and just take the first offer that came along. At least then she'd be out from under her father's thumb—

Except that with his wounded leg, he'd find some way to claim it her duty to look after him the rest of his life. *Honor your father and mother,* he'd say. She released a little sigh. There was no escape.

Did God really intend life to be so wretched? Papa would argue aye, that mankind was too sinful to expect anything else. Women were certainly too treacherous, and only their evil nature made them desire better.

Of course, her father did plenty of expecting better, himself. And made it her responsibility to see it happen.

Was that truly God's will?

With half the floor yet to do, she rose to her feet and carried the pail of dirty water out through the back door to toss in the yard, then walked to the spring to fetch a fresh one.

She'd just stooped to fill the pail when a man stepped from the thicket. Straightening, she gripped the pail as if it could protect her.

"Easy now," the man said, but did not move closer. A worn hat shaded dark eyes and mostly covered dark hair queued back.

"What do you want?"

"Information. And something to drink if it isn't too early."

"'Tis too early," she blurted. Then, "I have to finish scrubbing the floor. And my father and brothers are still asleep. But if you're quiet, and you're paying—"

He gave a quick nod. "I am indeed."

She filled the pail, still watching him, then allowing him to take it from her, led the way back to the tavern. As he set the pail down at the edge of where she'd left off scrubbing, she drew him a tankard of watered ale. "My thanks," he murmured, and sampled the brew while she withdrew to behind the counter.

He wiped his mouth with his sleeve and nodded his approval. "Very decent, especially in such difficult times."

She bobbed a nod in return.

"Now then. I believe you are acquainted with a certain Mr. Williams?"

The back of her neck prickled. "I am acquainted with several Mr. Williamses. To which do you refer?"

The man laughed softly and shook his head. "I think you know which one I mean. Did he leave any messages behind?"

Lizzy regarded the man in silence for a long moment. "Nay."

He squinted a little and took another sip of his ale. "Miss Cunningham, I am not your enemy."

All the warnings in her head were definitely at full cry now. "Enemy or nay, he did not leave a message."

He measured her in turn. "Very well." After tossing back the rest of the ale, he set the tankard down, put a pair of coins beside it, then pushed away from the counter.

"That's too much," Lizzy said.

The man smiled thinly. "Consider it my thanks for a bit of conversation."

"You should leave now." She lifted her chin. "My father doesn't take kindly to me speaking with men alone."

The smile widened. "I am safely married and no philanderer. Please give Mr. Williams my regards."

Her curiosity got the best of her. "Who should I say was inquiring?"

"Mr. Elliot." He hesitated and lowered his voice further. "Should you be in need of help, Miss

Cunningham, you may inquire for me at Dawson's Station, above Orangeburgh."

"Leave," she snapped, but quietly. "This instant."

A laugh was his parting reply. Lizzy snatched the coins off the counter, set the tankard on the shelf below, and whisked herself back to scrubbing before anyone could be the wiser.

A coldness settled deep in her belly and would not go away.

Chapter 7

Jed knew what battle looked like. This was nothing like it.

First order of the day had been for Cunningham to pay a visit to his former commanding officer, where the mischief of a pair of men going on ahead resulted in the old man being shot in his front yard, and Cunningham making a show of tears over it one minute, then in the next ordering the house to be burned, while the man's wife wept over his body.

'Twas all Jed could do not to ride off into the thicket and be sick.

They'd ridden north, then, to a place called Hayes Station. Galloped across a field in time to see all the men scramble into a blockhouse from where they'd loitered among the shops. Jed held Daisy back as far as he could from the stampede, but still he saw the leading riders chasing a pair of stragglers, one swinging his sword at the last as the blockhouse door closed. Shots answered from inside, and with a shout, Cunningham gave the order to take cover and return fire.

Jed's heart burned. All he could do was watch and deliberately misaim as he fired next to the others. With the whole company taken up by bloodlust, this was not the place to be giving his game away.

Kittery nudged him during a lull. "Time to use

that fancy rifle of your'n."

Jed shook his head and started to speak, but the cry went up that the blockhouse had been set on fire. Cunningham was in conversation with its occupants, and Jed could only half hear what was said.

"They'll be coming out directly." Kittery's eyes glittered. "The major will pick who he plans to execute. Others will be invited to step up and choose those they want particular vengeance against."

Sweat broke out over Jed's body, despite the cold. *Merciful God in heaven! What can I do here?*

Around him, men were leaving their hiding places and creeping closer, drawn by the promise of bloodshed. Jed swallowed and quickly reloaded his pistols, then followed, hanging back, yet an idea tickling the back of his brain.

It was mad. But if he fled, here and now, he'd never have another chance to make a difference.

The men inside the blockhouse trickled out, under a promise of mercy that there was no intention of honoring. Cunningham selected two and hanged them on a pole braced between two trees. The brother of one—barely more than a lad—flew forward, crying out in protest. Cunningham ordered the youth to be hanged as well, but the pole broke. In a fury, Cunningham fell upon them with his sword.

Jed turned away and shoved one of his pistols in his belt. He must remain cool. In the fray, his eyes fell upon the poor wretches stumbling out of the blockhouse, coughing, the building behind them consumed now with flames. Before any could stop him, he seized the shirt of one and hauled the man to his feet. "If you want to live, come with me," he growled, for the man's ears only, holding the other pistol to his temple.

A startled gaze came to his, and gaping, the man let himself be dragged along.

Basket tucked under her arm, shawl wrapped around her shoulders, Lizzy stepped carefully across the muddied road to the butcher's. After nearly a week of twitching at every little sound and having her heart nearly stop any number of times, she'd been told by Papa to expect extra patrons at the tavern tonight. And so they needed extra meat for a stew.

Supplies dwindled all the way around, though, and fast. How long they could continue operating, she did not know. Papa didn't seem concerned at all. Either he had sources she knew nothing of—of material goods as well as information, although she knew Dickie rode back and forth between her cousin Billy and the tavern—or he somehow expected their fortunes to change, even with the British having withdrawn to Charles Town.

They might even be forced to declare themselves rebel to keep making a living.

Her gut churned at the very thought. At the reminder of her suspicions, kindled at the visit of Mr. Elliot several days before. Suspicions which had done nothing but fester since.

She stepped through the door, nostrils pinching and stomach threatening to heave at the smell of blood and offal, and slid to the back of the room to wait for the three men already at the counter to finish their conversation. "—twenty-eight dead at Hayes Station," Mr. Foster, the butcher, said. "And before that, Captain Caldwell murdered in his own front yard."

Glancing her way, he fell silent, and as one they all turned to look at her. She swallowed. "If you please, I need—five pounds of beef."

Mr. Foster's chin came up, his eyes narrowing. "All out for today."

She knew better. "My coin's as good as anyone else's."

"Coin don't do you any good if I have no beef to sell."

Desperation choked her. "Look you, I cannot change my family's loyalties. But I've lived here most of my life, and I know each of you—your wives and children as well. I gladly serve all who come through our door, regardless of your own loyalty, and if you came to me in need—"

Richardson and Davis, the men on her side of the counter, seemed to loom over her of a sudden. She fought the urge to shrink back.

"Perhaps it is time you left, and gave the tavern tending over to someone less—oh, loyal," Richardson said.

Davis gave an ugly laugh.

She shot a glance at Mr. Foster and tried to keep the bitterness from her voice. "Thank you kindly for your time."

Keeping her face calm and her back straight, Lizzy retreated with as much dignity as she could muster.

She stomped all the way back to the tavern. They'd have to live with beans and a bit of salt beef tonight.

Why did her father continue to hang on here, anyway?

By the time she reached the sanctuary of her kitchen, she could hardly breathe, or see. She flung down the basket and her shawl, and gulping back a sob, swiped her apron across her eyes. They'd not reduce her to tears, those rebel bullyboys.

At least the soup of beans, rice, and salt beef cooked quickly enough, ready to serve by the time darkness fell and her cousin's company came wandering in. As the men whooped and jested between themselves, she kept her head down, meeting no one's gaze and seeking no one's attention. Not even—that one particularly troublesome new recruit.

As always, they treated her as invisible, boasting about such deeds the last few days as to turn her stomach completely. She understood their fury—did she not taste of rebel abuse barely an hour or so ago? But was this truly how to go about dealing with it?

Another burst of laughter, and the name she'd tried not to think of caught her ear. "Aye, and Williams here, he lost not one but two prisoners! What do you make of that?"

"I think he needs to wash the crockery this night, to learn him to work more carefully!"

More guffaws, and to her dim horror, Mr. Williams himself scraped his stool back and began gathering dishes. "An honorable enough occupation, I own," he replied with surprising cheer. "Seems I might as well, if I'm fit for nothing else."

She couldn't look away fast enough as he glanced across the crowded room at her and winked.

Familiar panic filled her chest. No refuge this time in the kitchen, for he headed that way, arms loaded with crockery to be washed.

But she couldn't leave him to smash it all, either, if he proved incapable of the task.

With a ragged sigh, she gathered her own armful and trudged after him.

Chapter 8

He'd hoped against hope that she'd follow him.

Not the slightest hint of softness in her demeanor, though, as she plunked her stacks of dirtied bowls and plates next to his and wiped her hands on her apron. "Do you truly know what to do with those? Besides break them, of course."

The grin stole across his face before he could stop it. "I've washed a tub or two of dishes in my time. I reckon I can keep from breaking them if need be."

Her bearing went beyond severe to openly hostile. He might be safer facing the troop out there in the common room. "Simpleton," she snapped, barely above a breath. "You might also want to have a care who you send asking for messages."

That doused any show of good cheer he might be able to summon.

"Aye. Look at me like you haven't an inkling what I mean. Your Mr. Elliot is like to get himself shot if he shows his face here again."

He still dared not move, dared not breathe. "So he did not get himself shot the first time."

She sustained the glare for a moment longer, then huffed and shook her head. "You men are all alike."

As she went to turn away, he stepped up close, blocking her way. "Nay. Not all."

Her gaze snapped to his, her expression going slack with shock. But she did not move.

That was progress.

"Did he come inside to find you, or…?"

A sharp shake of her head. "He surprised me at the spring. Then came in for a drink."

"Did he leave a message?"

Another shake, softer this time. "Only asked whether you had." She swallowed visibly. "Told me where to find him if—if I encountered trouble."

He nodded, glancing around to make sure no one had witnessed the exchange. Then he eased back, flashing her another smile. "Your dishwater is old. I'll fetch fresh from the spring."

Before she could stop him, he seized two pails from beside the door and ducked out into the night.

If Elliot had been there once, he might be again. Jed would risk it. He'd too much information to trust to the written word, or to—to Miss Cunningham. However much he might wish it.

He reached the spring, filled the pails, then set them down and waited. A slight rustle in the thicket set his pulse racing until Zach Elliot actually stepped into view. "Have a care with who you trust," he said, without preamble.

Jed set his hands on his hips. "I might say the same to you."

"Miss Cunningham is a tart one. I told her nothing of importance, but—watch yourself."

"Trying. 'Tis a bit difficult when she won't hold still long enough to let me even begin inquiring about her loyalties. But she trusts no one, especially not her own family."

They were keeping their voices low, but Elliot listened for a moment before replying. Only the wind in the pines came to Jed's ears.

"Do what you can, then," Elliot said. "And what news? I'm hearing some wild tales from the last few days."

Jed gave him a hurried summary of Cunningham's raids since Jed had been with him. The gathering concern on Elliot's face deepened.

"We should pull you if it's too dangerous—"

"I committed to doing this, and do this I will," Jed insisted. "Besides, I cannot go until I know if she can be persuaded to leave her father and brothers."

Elliot tucked his chin, peering at him in the half-dark. "Are you…soft on her?"

Half a dozen retorts tangled on his tongue. "I—there are things she's suffered at their hands, that I'd like to see an end to."

"Hmm." Elliot seemed unconvinced, but what did Jed care what the man thought?

Footsteps and a breathless feminine voice floated down the path. "Mr. Williams!"

"Aye, coming!" he called back, and gave a nod to Elliot as the man disappeared once more into the thicket.

He lifted both pails and made it halfway back before Miss Cunningham met him on the path. "Lost, Mr. Williams? There are dishes to be washed and men yet wanting their dinners."

Her chiding lacked much of the edge he was sure she intended.

In fact, if he did not miss his guess, that

breathlessness was—fear.

For him, or herself?

"It took longer to fetch water than I expected," he said.

"Indeed."

He made to move past her, but she stayed in the middle of the path. He glanced around, listening, but it seemed they were alone. "Is aught amiss?" he murmured, for her ears alone.

"What are you doing?" she whispered fiercely.

"Naught for you to be concerned about." He tried a smile, but her expression did not change. "Corresponding with someone about family. Back home."

"Your family cast you out." She edged closer. "Or did they?"

Silence was likely his greatest ally in the moment.

"You," she breathed, "are a filthy rebel. Are you not?"

He leaned toward her till a bare handspan lay between their noses. "That's a grave offense to accuse a man of, in this place."

"*Are* you?"

Starlight glimmered in her eyes. Her half-parted lips trembled. The scent of something clean and wholesome washed over him—

A good thing, likely, that both of his hands were busy holding pails of water. He straightened and gave her another smile. "Excuse me, Miss Cunningham. There are dishes to be washed."

And with that, he brushed past her.

~*~*~*~

How had he done that? So neatly managed to evade answering and then flash that grin as if he could slide by on charm alone, and leave her so completely without words—

Lizzy gritted her teeth as she followed him back to the tavern. Ignored the hoots and jeers at them emerging from the darkness together. What did she care what they thought?

Inside, he was already pouring water into a kettle and hanging it over the kitchen fire, then he tackled the dishes she'd left stacked in the old water.

As she'd thought. Not so used-up, after all. Merely a pretext for him to walk to the spring.

He glanced up and caught her watching him, angled her a half smile and kept washing. With a huff, she found a cloth and took up the task of wiping dry a stack of earthenware bowls.

They worked in silence, settling into a surprisingly comfortable rhythm, even as the common room became more unruly. The call went out for more ale, and her unexpected helper for the evening lifted a staying hand and carried out a pair of pitchers himself, answering the other men's teasing with his own laughter and jests. In the kitchen, Lizzy kept working, listening to his easy way with them all.

If he was a rebel, in truth, he hid it well. She could not reconcile his manner at this moment—nor his kindness to her—with what she'd witnessed earlier at the butcher's.

Of course, there were likely wretches on both

sides of the conflict. Honorable men, too, possibly.

She snorted. Less likely, that.

"Thinking disparaging thoughts about me again, Miss Cunningham?"

She startled at the low voice just behind her—despite the effort not to—and twitched to find him *right there.* Blue eyes sparkling in the lamplight, which traced a warm gold from the strands of his hair falling messily out of its queue. Shoulders impossibly broad in his simple shirt and waistcoat—

"Aye." She shoved her hands back into the dishwater, scrubbing at something she knew was coloration of the earthenware and not a stain. "Always."

His chuckle gusted across her. Drew a sting to her eyes and an ache to her throat. Why, she could not say.

"Likely I deserve it well enough." He lifted the cloth and set to the drying.

She peeked at him from the corner of her eye, found his expression unexpectedly somber. "Why would you say that?"

His smile this time was sad. "Have all men of your acquaintance been so slow to acknowledge their own unworthiness?"

She sniffed again. "Oh, they avow their worth most strenuously, lest I forget."

He did not immediately reply to that. "Miss Cunningham," he began, then hesitated.

"Lizzy," she muttered.

She felt rather than saw his stillness, felt herself growing warm under the weight of his gaze.

"Oh, come now, I know you've heard the others call me by my given name."

"I," he said, quietly but firmly, "am not the others. And I hope most sincerely that you do not feel I am."

He moved away to fetch the now-warmed fresh water and pour some into the washtub, then nudged her aside. "My turn again." Another quick smile. "Lizzy."

Too shocked to resist, she let him take over, numbly reaching for the dampened drying cloth. Where was her tongue?

And how could her name sound so nearly like a caress on his?

As her cheeks flamed, she ducked away under the pretext of arranging clean tankards on a tray.

"I'm Jed," came his low voice, tugging her back around.

"Jed?"

"Short for Jedidiah."

A solid name for a solid man. "It suits you."

Now where had that come from?

His gaze held hers. "And Lizzy is short for—Elizabeth?"

Her face must be positively crimson by now. "Aye," she said faintly.

"Lovely," he said, unmoving. "The name and—the girl who wears it."

Lightning swept through her, head to toe. Her mouth opened, but no sound would come out.

Suddenly he was there, using the cloth in her hands to dry his own, so close she could feel the warmth from his body. His knuckles came up to brush her chin.

Still she could not move.

What in blazes was wrong with her?

A frown knitted his brows. “Has no one ever told you that? Truly?”

She shook her head a little. His eyes held her captive, and his fingers slid across her jaw, toward her ear—

And then—he was kissing her. Everything inside her melted.

Chapter 9

He should not—he really shouldn't. Not without knowing where she stood, if she was willing to defend him once he was able to tell her the truth. But the disbelief in her face, the shattered look in those eyes…

Would she believe him now, or would it only seem that he was taking advantage?

For half a breath, she stiffened, then almost imperceptibly leaned into him.

It was the sweetest kiss he'd ever taken—or given.

He forced himself to pull back. This time, awe glistened in her eyes. Still touching her cheek, and the other hand holding hers tangled in the drying cloth, he decided to risk all. "Tell me, Lizzy. If you had opportunity to leave here…would you?"

Confusion flickered across the features that were, aye, truly lovely.

How had he not seen it before?

"What do you mean? What else is there, besides fleeing to Charles Town like any common refugee?"

He smiled. "I made a very respectable living, before—before the rebellion. I reckon I could do so again. You'd not have to live as a refugee if I had anything to say about it."

Watching the shift of light and feeling in her

eyes—suspicion, doubt, hope—*please say aye,* he wanted to beg. And with every beat his heart echoed, *aye, aye, aye…*

"Well, this is a pretty sight, to be sure," came a voice.

Lizzy's father stood in the doorway.

What a blasted idiot he was for letting himself be caught.

Lizzy wrenched away, eyes wide, cheeks scarlet, then pale. Jed made up his mind then and there to play the game as far as he could, for her sake if nothing else.

The older man's gaze was narrowed, calculating, as it swept between his daughter and Jed. The corner of his mouth lifted. "I should ask you, Mr. Williams, just what is your intent here with my daughter?"

"We were only washing dishes, Papa," she said, but Jed waved a hand in her direction, hoping she caught the signal to let him speak.

"My intent, Mr. Cunningham," he said, clearing his throat, "is to win your daughter. Honorably."

He sent her a look, hoping, pleading—

The color rose in her cheeks again, though not as sharply as before. "You are daft as well as a simpleton."

He laughed. He couldn't help it. "Perhaps."

"Why would you want Lizzy?" Mr. Cunningham sounded genuinely puzzled. "She ain't much to look at. Suppose she's a decent enough cook and housekeeper—though you must know I won't brook her leaving her aged papa behind." His expression grew sharp again. "A pair of strong hands to run the tavern might be welcome enough."

Jed forced himself to a semblance of proper respect and interest. "I just want Lizzy," he said, then prayed the older man would not feel the veiled threat he found himself putting behind the words.

Halfway across the kitchen, Lizzy put a hand over her mouth.

"I want her safe, and happy," he added.

Head tipped, Mr. Cunningham regarded him as he might an interesting insect. "We will see," he said at last, then nodded toward the common room. "Lizzy, we need more ale."

"We're nearly out," she said, in a small voice.

He halted midturn and shot her a glare. Flicked a glance at Jed. "Ale, or mulled cider, or something, then, girl. You know your work. Get to it!"

And with that, he lumbered back to the common room. Jed released a long breath.

Lizzy rounded on him. "Why? Why would you say that?"

He really wanted nothing more than to swoop her into his arms and kiss her again. Longer this time. That impulse must be contained, however, along with the wild grin tugging at his mouth. She needed to know how serious he truly was about all this.

That above all, he was not trifling with her affections.

He took a measured step toward her. "Because…I meant it."

She backed away, shaking her head, gaze darting everywhere but at his face. "How—how can you? You heard my father—I'm nothing to look at—"

He gave into the impulse at least in part, and caught her into his arms. "Only because no one has stopped long enough to truly look."

When he tried tipping her chin up, she resisted him. "I'd never be able to escape him," she murmured, her voice mournful. "He'll let you near me only for your help keeping the tavern."

Slipping his hand around the back of her neck, he pressed his lips to her forehead. She felt damp and feverish, all at once. "Your father has your brothers, if it comes to that. Unless you want to stay and keep the tavern?"

Another small head shake, but she was beginning to lose her stiffness in his embrace. "I don't think we'll be able to stay."

He kissed her forehead again. She smelled delightful. "They're determined to chase all loyalists out of the backcountry, aren't they?"

"Aye." She softened against him another fraction, then gave his chest a halfhearted shove. "I need to see what else we have to offer for drink."

Not letting go, he nuzzled her hair. "It can wait another minute."

"You don't know my father."

He huffed. "True. But his kind, I know well enough." Reluctantly he released her. "So, what is this about nearly being out of ale?"

A kettle of warmed cider and half a keg of watered ale later, the common room began to empty and Lizzy retired to the kitchen to tend the last washtub of dishes while Jed swept and tidied elsewhere. Papa finally went upstairs to bed as her cousin's men wandered outside to sleep, but not before a final glare and growl about tending her chores.

Not a word about Jed, however. Lizzy winced to think what he'd have to say about that once Jed was away with the other men, tomorrow.

Robert drifted into the kitchen and poked around the pantry. "Anything left to eat?"

"Nay," she said, without turning around.

He sniffed. "I'm thinking of riding out with Cousin Billy in the morning."

Good riddance if so. "That would be too much like work for you, wouldn't it?"

Her brother snickered. "What, just because I don't do the washing and sweeping—like your sweetheart out there—you think I couldn't handle it?"

Lizzy slid him a glance. Did everyone know, already?

On the other hand, did she mind?

Robert pulled an apple from the bin at the bottom of the pantry, rubbed it on his shirt, and took a bite. "Is he truly your sweetheart? I didn't figure Williams for being a lackwit, or blind." He grinned at his own humor. "Or are you finally givin' up what you never let anyone else have? What's he promised you, for that?"

"He's kind," she muttered into the dishwater. "Something that never occurred to you, I'm sure."

He sauntered toward her. "You think you're pretty smart, don't you, Lizzy?"

"If I was, you'd let me know."

She tried to keep her voice mild, Lord help her, she did. Would Robert keep his hands to himself while Jed was still in the building? Or—worse—would he bide his time and try to catch her later?

Sniggering again, he edged up close to her. "I could be kind."

She stilled her hands in the dishwater. "Step off, Robbie."

"What, you gonna scream for your sweetheart?" He lifted the apple and took another bite, up close to her ear. So close she could feel his breath and smell his stench. "I wager you won't. Papa would beat you if you caused a ruckus."

Lizzy gritted her teeth. So tempting to fling—

"I'll beat you if *you* cause one," came a low voice behind them.

Robert scrambled away, trying yet to appear cool. Jed stood there, thunder in his face like Lizzy hadn't guessed he was capable of, the broom held crosswise in his hands like a weapon. "Lizzy, he touch you?"

Heart pounding, she shook her head.

Jed took a step toward her brother, who'd gone pale, the apple dangling from his fingers. "Let's get one thing straight, here. I aim to see your sister cared for, whether that's here or elsewhere. If any of you lays one hand on her, you'll answer to me. Is that understood?"

Robert nodded, then sidled around the edge of the room and scurried away.

Lizzy blew out a breath and turned back to the washtub. Jed set the broom against the wall next to the table. "Are you well, in truth?" he breathed.

Eyes stinging, she couldn't bring herself to look at him. And her heart was still like to climb up into her throat. She managed a quick nod.

"Lizzy?"

From the corner of her eye, she saw his hand, outstretched.

If she let him hold her, 'twould be the end of her composure—

But she wanted it. God forgive her, she did.

She dove into his arms and let his strength wrap her about.

"Shh, it'll be all right," he murmured into her hair.

Hardly knowing where to put her hands, she gripped the back of his shoulders and pressed her face into his chest. "Please—" The word came out strangled, but she had to ask. "Please don't go with my cousin tomorrow."

His breath caught. "Oh, Lizzy."

"Please."

One hand smoothed from the crown of her head to the small of her back. "I must," he whispered.

She twitched away, swallowing back the sudden ache at the loss of that warmth, and gave him her best glare. "You—you claim to not be like them. And yet you tell me you must?"

His eyes were shadowed, full of secrets and—a tenderness that would surely break her. "Aye." He reached up to brush the side of her face. "Do you not think your cousin's cause true and right?"

"I—" The reply clogged her throat. "I don't know."

Both hands came up to frame her face, and he

studied her gravely. "I think you do know. Your asking me not to go is its own judgment against them, whether you realize it or not."

"My asking you not to go"—she gulped back the tears— "is purely selfish." She blinked, looked away, tried to pull back again. "Never you mind. I've borne worse—"

"Lizzy." Jed bent closer, capturing her attention once more. "Do you think your cousin is likely to stop his careening all over the backcountry unless he's forced to?"

Time slowed, then stopped. Her heartbeat became painful.

His eyes held her, like bits of the summer sky, willing her to—what? She could hardly think with him so near.

"Nay," she breathed. "Likely not."

Inexplicably, he smiled. "Then trust me when I say I must go."

What—*oh!* The implication of his words crashed over her like a storm's flood on the river. "Nay—oh, nay," she whimpered.

His arms gathered her in as she buried her face against his shoulder. The beating of his heart under her cheek echoed the raging of her thoughts.

"You know what he does to anyone who tries to naysay him," she said, trying to keep her voice quiet. "He'll kill you."

"He can try," Jed rumbled. "I've good reason now not to throw my life away." His embrace tightened. "And I promise you, while there's breath left in my body, I'll either send for you, or come myself. Can you trust me with that much?"

The weeping took her, finally. "He won't let you live," was all she could manage.

The heaving breath under her cheek told her he knew the truth of it. "If you can't trust me with it, then at least trust the Almighty."

She rolled her head back and forth. "Why would God listen to me? Why would He not just send me more pain—"

The old anger rose, and with it, a comfortingly familiar strength, however bitter. She wrenched out of his arms and stepped back.

"Lizzy—"

"Nay." She had to distance herself from him. From the hurt.

Which already dug so deep that she couldn't see, couldn't breathe. He'd told her he cared for her welfare—kissed her—made her believe there might be more to her life than eternal servitude to her father and brothers—and now this?

She shook her head, throwing a last hopeless glance at Jed. His blue eyes shone with sadness.

"Nay. I'll not stand by and watch you be murdered." And then she fled.

Knowing he surely would bring perdition down on his head, in the form of her cousin's wrath, no less—her only refuge was in returning to not caring.

If only she'd never cared at all.

Chapter 10

Just that quickly, he'd lost her.

And once again, she'd run from him, as if he were her enemy.

Which he was, in technical terms, but—having her hurry off to tell someone was not his fear now, oddly enough.

He caught himself still staring at the empty doorway of the kitchen long after the sound of her footsteps had faded, up the stairs, across the hall and up to her own room. Scrubbed both hands across his face, then set to finishing up the washing. 'Twas the least he could do.

Lord—oh Lord—

The prayer faltered against the memory of her wounded fury. All he'd meant to do was tell her to have faith, and she'd flung it back in his face as if he'd asked her to do something vile.

But after seeing firsthand how both father and brother treated her, could he blame her for being too cautious to hope?

Keep protecting her, Lord. Please. And I ask again—if it please You, bring me back to her.

As if in response, a snippet of Scripture floated through his thoughts. Elbows on the edge of the washtub, he sank until his forehead rested on his dripping fists.

Please, Lord. I beg you. Do not let this hope

disappoint her.

A creak came from the common room, and heavy footsteps after. "Williams? You here?"

Blast it. "Aye. Washing up."

The tall form of Major Cunningham filled the doorway, a sly smile curling his mouth. "Well, well. Our Lizzy truly has you snared?"

Jed snorted and kept at the task. Ignored the prickling at the back of his neck as Cunningham sauntered closer.

"So, are you with us, or nay?"

"I am with you."

"Are you sure?" Cunningham leaned against the wall.

Jed gave him a long look. "Why would I not be?"

The other man chuckled, affecting a casualness Jed was sure he did not feel. "No particular reason, except my uncle seems to think you bear watching." The teasing grin turned feral. "Our Lizzy is a good girl. She'll do whatever my uncle deems best."

Jed swished the water in search of the last piece of crockery. "I only want what is best for her."

"Hmm. That's admirable enough."

Admirable? Jed lifted his head and met Cunningham's mocking gaze. This man wanted to discuss what was admirable?

"I tell you, though," Cunningham went on, "riding with us is likely safer than staying and facing Lizzy's tongue."

"I'm not afraid of Lizzy." Jed hefted the washtub and angled for the back door.

Cunningham's laughter gusted after him. "You

should be!"

The next day dawned cold and blustery, but Cunningham insisted they move on before full daylight. Jed was half surprised they hadn't been attacked during the night, but perhaps there hadn't yet been enough time for the intelligence he'd given Elliot to have its effect.

Jed could feel the hostility from the settlement's other inhabitants, though no one dared to speak or do aught against Cunningham's company. He glanced across the sea of green coats mixed with hunting shirts—like his own, and the occasional blanket-swathed form, both Indian and white, some mounted but some waiting beside their horses for the call to move out. Daisy shifted beneath him, and he patted her absently, then sent a glance for the hundredth time to the attic window of the tavern. The shutter lay ajar but no movement could he glimpse behind.

Lizzy had not come downstairs as they'd prepared to leave, either. They snatched a few bites of cold rations—not that she could have baked anything that would satisfy such a large group, with provisions as they were. The soup she'd prepared the day before had been miraculous, under the circumstances. How they continued to operate the tavern with so little—

He shook his head. Enough gazing up at her window. He had to at least try for a proper farewell.

Dismounting, he handed his reins to Kittery.

"Hold her. I'll be back in a moment."

He threaded his way through the other riders, to the tavern's back door, skirting the knot of men that included the Cunninghams, deep in conversation. Inside, he stopped and listened, and when no sound came to his ears, made his way as quietly as possible upstairs and through the hallway to the attic steps.

The narrow door at the top was closed. As it should be. And hopefully barred. He tiptoed upward and listened at the wood. A soft scuffing came from somewhere inside.

He rapped softly. "Lizzy? Lizzy, 'tis me, Jed."

A definite sniffle this time. "Go away."

Of course. "Not until you hear me out. Please."

A rustling came to the door, and stopped, but she did not open it.

He let out a breath and spread his hand against the rough planks. "I'm praying for you, Lizzy. Have been praying, and I won't stop. Not until—until I'm back, and you're in my arms again." The ache that had lodged his chest since last night began to ease, just a little, at saying the words. "And—I'd be honored if you'd consider that a proposal of marriage. With or without your father's approval."

A sliding sound, and a thump on the other side, but still she did not open.

Not that he expected it.

Maybe he really was a fool.

With a rueful smile, he patted the door. "Be well, Lizzy. And trust the Almighty."

The ache grew again as he retreated down the steps and outside. The Cunninghams had scattered, with both father and son staring when he emerged from the tavern's back door. Jed stared calmly back. Lizzy's father held his gaze, but the brother glanced away.

He made his way back to Kittery and Daisy and swung into the saddle. This time, the attic shutter opened a little more, nudged by a slender hand—all he could see of the shadow hovering there. Jed waved her a salute and took his place with the column as it moved out.

In the press of horses and riders, Bill Cunningham circled his mount and sidled up to Jed's. His green regimentals were brilliant against the morning grey. "So you've decided to join us after all?"

Jed kept his face impassive, but he gave a determined nod. "I said that I would."

Major Cunningham laughed and clapped him on the shoulder, addressing the company at large. "This one aspires to tame our Lizzy! Think he's worthy of the task?"

Jed's ears and cheeks burned at the guffaws and quips rising in the wake of this pronouncement.

"Tame, or be tamed?" one called out, and another wave of laughter followed. "I'd say the latter, after watching him help her keep tavern last night."

"Aye, well, if he aspires to join himself to our family, he'd best prove himself, hadn't he?"

Chapter 11

If Lizzy thought a week could be interminable before, it was doubly so now.

The first day of December came and went with no word from either her cousin's company, Jed himself, or Mr. Elliot.

Maybe she'd simply dreamed it all. Because that's surely all it could be, with a man who not only told her she was lovely but threatened Robbie with bodily harm on her behalf…then asked her to be his.

Or else he'd said those things merely to gain her trust, and never intended to make good on them.

Be well, Lizzy. And trust the Almighty.

She was as well as she could be. But she didn't know how to begin accomplishing the other.

Papa stood out front in the cool sunshine, arguing with Mr. Foster for the fourth time this week. Likely trying to convince their neighbors he meant nothing by hosting her cousin and his company of men. With each passing day, the reports that trickled back to them were more difficult to believe.

She would not let herself think about Jed in the middle of all that. She would not—

And her heart was such a liar.

Peeking out to ensure Papa and the butcher were still deep in conversation, she snatched up her shawl and hurried out the back door of the tavern. Ducking behind the necessary, she cut through the thicket before reemerging on the path.

'Twasn't far to the church, and hopefully she'd be back before Papa noticed she was gone.

Thankfully, she met no one on the road, and soon the small log building came into view through the South Carolina forest. No one appeared to be there, but the door was unbarred.

Pushing the door open, she slid inside, then stood still, breathing deeply. The place smelled damply of pine. She'd not been here in, oh, so long she could hardly remember. They'd not had a regular minister in years, and the exchange minister came but once every couple of months or so. But as she recalled, a worn Bible lay on pulpit.

God in heaven, are you here? And do you see me?

She crept forward. There—aye—lay the Bible, illuminated by a faint pool of light from a small, high window nearby.

Another deep breath, and she walked the rest of the way, between the rows of bench seats and up three steps into the pulpit. Her fingers brushed the dusty leather cover. Where to begin?

Wedging her fingertips somewhere in the middle, she opened the book and smoothed the pages back. *The Song of songs, which is Solomon's,* she read. *Let him kiss me with the kisses of his mouth: for thy love is better than wine—*

"Oh, for pity's sake!" She couldn't turn the pages fast enough. Who knew something like that was in the Holy Scriptures? Not helpful in the least.

Psalms. That should be better. *O LORD God of hosts, how long wilt thou be angry against the prayer of thy people? Thou feedest them with the bread of tears; and givest them tears to drink in great measure. Thou makest us a strife unto our neighbors: and our enemies laugh among themselves. Turn us again, O God of hosts, and cause thy face to shine; and we shall be saved.*

Much better. But still not quite what her heart was longing for.

Perhaps the New Testament.

The thief cometh not, but for to steal, and to kill, and to destroy: I am come that they might have life, and that they might have it more abundantly. I am the good shepherd: the good shepherd giveth his life for the sheep....

Further in. *Let brotherly love continue. Be not forgetful to entertain strangers: for thereby some have entertained angels unawares.... Marriage is honourable in all... Let your conversation be without covetousness; and be content with such things as ye have: for he hath said, I will never leave thee, nor forsake thee. So that we may boldly say, The LORD is my helper, and I will not fear what man shall do unto me.*

She stopped, considered the words again. *I will never leave thee, nor forsake thee.*

A quick turn of pages backwards. *Call unto me, and I will answer thee, and show thee great and mighty things, which thou knowest not.*

Call unto me... great and mighty things...

A few more pages back. *For I know the thoughts that I think toward you, saith the LORD, thoughts of peace, and not of evil, to give you an expected end. Then shall ye call upon me, and ye shall go and pray unto me, and I will hearken unto you. And I will be found of you, saith the LORD: and I will turn away your captivity...*

...thoughts of peace, and not of evil. An expected end.

I will hearken unto you.

She sank to the floor, covering her face with her shawl.

Oh, Lord God, could it be true? You think of me? And You hear me?

She'd not let the tears overcome her since that night Jed had kissed and held her so sweetly—though they'd tried often enough, to be sure—but she could not stop them now. Nor the memories—Jed's lips on hers, surprisingly warm and soft against the slight rasp of his chin—his blue eyes, entreating—the rumble of his voice as he exhorted her to trust God.

If You are there—if You hear me truly—then keep him safe through this madness of my cousin's. And...if it is not too presumptuous of me...bring him back...to me.

The Scripture flitted through her thoughts again, *Let him kiss me with the kisses of his mouth...*

Heat swept through her, and she sank even lower.

Oh God...if my thoughts are unworthy, forgive me. But Your Holy Scriptures said it. Is it wrong, then, to wish for the love of a good man?

~*~*~*~

Wrapped in his blanket, Jed huddled against the gnarled trunk of a live oak, alternately watching the twinkle of stars in the cold night sky through the branches and the array of campfires a short distance away. In spite of the recent snow, and partly in thanks to the fact that live oaks did not shed their leaves until new ones budded in spring, he'd found a relatively bare, dry spot under its branches and laid claim to it before anyone else could. Most of the other men huddled around the fires, but Jed felt snug and protected here. After nearly a month of pretending he belonged, he had no taste this night for conversation and jesting.

More than a week ago, Major Cunningham and the other commanding officer had divided the company and gone their separate ways to continue finding such mischief as they could. Pursuit by the rebels had become more direct, and some of Cunningham's stragglers had been captured and hung at a crossroads shortly after they'd left Lizzy's tavern. Jed wasn't sure whether to be grateful or not that he'd escaped such a fate simply because Cunningham had kept him close. He'd not had opportunity to slip away and send a message to Elliot, either.

The longer he stayed with Cunningham's outfit, the more despondent he felt—and the closer he felt nudged toward the edge of committing something he'd never be able to justify, regardless of how it might contribute to the bloody major's downfall.

True to his word, Cunningham had indeed held him under his watchful eye. After the departure of

Colonel Williams and his troops, Cunningham had further divided his own remaining men into two groups, sending one farther up the backcountry with the intent to hide out among the Cherokee nation. All left were those willing to return to Charles Town, if necessary.

They'd moved often, rarely camping in the same place twice, but mostly around the upper forks of the Edisto River. Once or twice Jed had caught a glimpse of Lizzy's brother—not the one he'd threatened, but the one she'd said often rode back and forth between their tavern and Major Cunningham. Carrying supplies and intelligence both ways, unless Jed missed his guess. Her brother had glanced his direction but not acknowledged him. Just enough for Jed to know he was aware of Jed's presence, but an obvious cut.

The man was gone before Jed could make his way over to him. Not that he cared, but Jed would have liked to inquire after Lizzy's welfare.

The ache in his chest at the thought of her had grown no less sharp. As always, he tried at least to pour it into prayer for her—in between prayers for his own presence here to have some good purpose.

It didn't help that desperation hung about the camp in a nearly palpable cloud. Cunningham himself had grown surly. Kittery and the other men whispered that he'd nearly run out of men to cut down. Some feared he'd start in on his own.

Jed just might be the first, if it came to that.

He settled himself more comfortably against the oak. Having prayed until he felt fair exhausted, he closed his eyes and let his thoughts drift toward his one consolation these days, after prayer itself—the memory of the fiery girl who for a few, sweet moments, actually trusted him enough to let him hold her in his arms.

Chapter 12

Lizzy woke from a dream of endless requests for whiskey to shouts and the flicker of torches through her half-shuttered window.

And pounding on the wall at the foot of the attic stairs. "Lizzy! Wake up!"

She bolted out of bed and peered through the shutter. Half the settlement looked to be in their front yard.

"Now, Lizzy! They're going to burn the place!"

Lightning spurted through her veins. With no more thought, she seized various things from around the room and flung them into the middle of her bed, gathered all into a bundle, and wrapped herself in her shawl, then shoved her feet into her shoes.

Robbie was waiting for her at the far end of the hallway, beckoning for her to hurry. "Dickie's already downstairs with Papa."

"What madness is this?"

"Blasted rebels. They've decided to punish us for Cousin Bill's adventures."

He didn't offer to carry her bundle—not that it was much—but at least he'd wakened her and made sure she got out. "Fortunate they've let us come away with our lives," she muttered, as they sped down the stairs.

"So far," Robbie said.

"Not comforting in the least."

The common room was already in flames, and Robbie tugged her out the back door. A pair of men stood by the stable, their faces menacing in the torchlight. Richardson and Davis, from the butcher shop that one day. She hesitated. What if she just slipped away into the thicket, made her way to Dawson's Station, and left her father and brothers to their own fate?

"Get along, missie," Davis said, with a grin and point of his musket. "Stay with the rest of the vermin you call family."

She gritted her teeth. "I'd rather not."

Their sneers deepened. "Rather too late to turn coat now, Lizzy Cunningham. Go on with you, now."

With a huff, she followed after Robert. *Oh God, hear my plea. Help me. Preserve me—*

"My Lizzy! Oh, thank the good Lord you're safe."

The false affection in her father's cry soured her stomach, but she let herself be nudged closer to him, on the far edge of the yard. A good heat rose from the blaze of the tavern at her back.

"You four." Mr. Foster, the butcher, addressed them, the flames glinting off his spectacles. "We've been as forbearing as we could, but your harboring the sorest of Tory scourges ever to plague the backcountry can no longer go unanswered. Consider yourself hereby stripped of all possession in the United States of America."

"Where are we supposed to go?" her father demanded.

"I suggest Charles Town, with the rest of your royalist cronies, to await whatever transportation the Crown deems fit."

Her father chewed his lip for a moment, then spread his hands in a beseeching gesture. "Have pity on us." Lizzy cringed at the whine in his voice. "For years now we've given you all good service—"

"We do have pity." Mr. Foster's gaze went to Lizzy, chilling her through despite the fury behind it. "You're allowed to depart with your lives and whatever you can carry."

She drew a deep breath, and while her father continued to sputter, lifted her head and set out upon the road in the direction of Orangeburgh, and it was to be supposed, Charles Town.

~*~*~*~

Hours later, near dawn, her father begged for a stop.

A half mile down the road, Lizzy had taken the time to dress more properly, then tied the bundle of what was left across her back with her shawl. Her father and the boys trailed behind, Dickie complaining that they'd not even let him take his horse, and her father leaning on Robbie's arm. She trudged ahead, acknowledging none of them.

They could follow her, or not. She was determined to find Mr. Elliot and throw herself on his mercy.

"Shouldn't we be going south to the Edisto?" Dickie asked, but Papa shushed him.

Lizzy gritted her teeth. Tempting it was to seek

out her cousin and thus hopefully Jed…but if she understood Jed's intended purpose aright, they'd best be nowhere near her cousin and his men.

"My feet are freezing," her father complained.

Lizzy unclenched her jaw enough to reply, "We're nearly to Dawson's Station. You can warm yourself there."

"Insolent chit," he growled.

She walked faster.

Pines and bare-limbed sweet gum and oak towered over the road. Through the branches, the sky gradually lightened, helping her forget her own feet and hands, aching with the cold. At least the weather had cleared. If they'd chosen to burn the tavern during that snow a week ago—

Lizzy's eyes stung. Their tavern. The home she remembered best since her childhood. The attic room, her only haven since Mama's death years ago.

God, what do you have for me now? What will I find at the end of this road?

Part of her longed to just lie down, close her eyes, and never open them again.

Be well, Lizzy.

She let her lids slide closed. Kept putting one foot in front of the other.

"He won't let you live," she'd cried out.

Trust, came the reply, strong and nearly audible against the deep winter silence.

I want to, her heart answered. *But if Jed does not survive—*

She could not bear thinking of the alternative.

Please, Lord. Please.

Dawson's Station lay a mere fifteen miles from her father's tavern, but this felt like a journey from one lifetime to another.

Perhaps it was.

The sun peeked over the horizon, through the trees, as the cluster of log buildings came into sight—a blockhouse, a trading post, and another tavern much like their own. Lizzy stopped to resettle her burden across her shoulders and rubbed her eyes before trudging on to the tavern, ignoring the racing of her heart.

The shock and necessity of the past hours had worn thoroughly off. She was weary beyond bearing, looked a fright, she was sure, and likely still smelled of smoke. But, this was it. She'd never again return home. Not if she could help it.

She knocked at the tavern door. A shuttered window opened above and a man peered down, hair loose past his shoulders. "What is it at this hour?"

"Please, is a Mr. Elliot here?" She tried to keep her voice hushed. "I need to speak with him."

The man's sleepy glare softened a fraction. "Who might I tell him is inquiring?"

She glanced back at the road. Her father and brothers were just now catching up. "A friend of—Mr. Williams. If you please."

With a last severe, searching look, he gave a quick nod and disappeared. Lizzy blew out a breath and, after shedding her bundle, collapsed onto the bench beside the door.

Papa limped into the yard, supported by Robbie.

Oh, God... Any prayer she had at this point was inarticulate.

The door was unbarred from within and swung open. Lizzy stood as Mr. Elliot stepped out, his haste evident in his own unbound hair and absence of waistcoat over shirt and breeches. But he held his rifle at the ready. "Miss Cunningham, this is a surprise."

"Please." She was not above begging if need be, not in this case. "Our Whig neighbors burned the tavern. We'd nowhere to go now but Charles Town, but—I'm here to ask your mercy."

He seemed to understand the plea in her words—and in her eyes—for he nodded slowly.

Her father's shuffling footsteps announced his approach. "Lizzy, fool girl, step out of the way and let me have that seat—"

She sidled away, still watching Mr. Elliot as he assessed the three men trailing her. Papa dropped to the bench with a huff and cast his own glare about.

"Does your request include them?" Mr. Elliot asked.

She chewed her lip. How even to say it?

Turning to face her father and brothers, she squared her shoulders and lifted her chin. "You may all go on to Charles Town without me. After a suitable rest, of course."

Her brothers gaped, but Papa surged to his feet once more, leaning on his staff, eyes narrowed and face reddening. "What's the meaning of this, Lizzy?"

She stepped back and folded her hands in front of her. "I'm not going with you, Papa."

Lord help her, she tried to hold herself still, to brace for whatever he might do, and still his anger took her by surprise. He lunged and backhanded her, moving so fast she'd not time to dodge.

She stumbled and fell.

"None of that!" Mr. Elliot roared, and hauled Papa up by the back of his coat. Papa swung his staff but Mr. Elliot caught it and wrenched it away. "Dawson! Lend a hand here."

The other man was already there, and between the two they subdued Papa while Lizzy picked herself up out of the frozen mud.

Papa stood shaking, alternating between cursing Lizzy and demanding Dickie and Robbie do something. Both edged back, eyes wide, clutching the small bundles they'd managed to carry away with them as well.

Mr. Elliot addressed them tightly. "There's still time to make honorable men of yourselves. But choose—either continue to Charles Town, as your sister suggests, or reconsider your loyalties and apply yourselves to making a new life here. I warn you, however, the time is fast approaching that there'll be no room for wavering."

Robert gaped like a fish, opening and closing his mouth. Dickie went completely white, and turned and fled down the road.

"He's bound to go warn my cousin," Lizzy murmured to Mr. Elliot.

Other men had emerged, in varying states of undress, to see what the ruckus was. With a word from Mr. Elliot, several of them apprehended Dickie, and Robert surrendered without a fight. In short order all three Cunningham men were dragged away to gaol.

Suddenly without strength, Lizzy sat down on the bench again.

"Are you well?"

She looked up to find Mr. Elliot bending a concerned frown upon her.

"I—" Her cheek hurt where Papa had struck her, and a wave of dizziness overcame her. "Well enough."

His frown did not waver.

With a sigh, she drew herself up. "My brother has been communicating with my cousin. I heard him mention going to him, south, on the Edisto River. I—I think they must be camped there?"

Mr. Elliot's dark eyes shone. "Thank you. It's a brave thing you've done, coming here."

She could only blink at him.

"Come," he said. "Mistress Dawson will be glad to see to you. Then we can discuss what happens next."

Chapter 13

December deepened until Jed could no longer remember what day it was. Christmas neared, but how closely was anyone's guess. Even Kittery could not recall.

Cunningham had further divided the company and scattered them in camps all up and down both branches of the Edisto River, in groups of twenty or so. Predictably, he'd kept Jed with him.

At least they'd not been out on any more killing raids, since leaving Lizzy's tavern. But Cunningham grew more restive by the day, as if bloodshed was a kind of craving for him.

A craving for which Cunningham would soon find satisfaction by Jed's own blood, he was sure.

Lord in heaven, have mercy...

'Twas nearly all he could pray, anymore.

He lay curled in his blanket in the predawn grey, eyes open even before he was fully awake, listening to early morning on the river—as he did every morning of late. The stamp and muted snort of horses, the rustle of men just beginning to stir about. The occasional cry of a winter bird, if the weather were quiet.

When the first shots sounded, upriver, he was on his feet without thought, rifle in hand. Others did the same. "It's an attack!" someone shouted.

Jed grabbed his gear, grateful he hadn't

unpacked much the night before. He seized his saddle and cinched it down, then swung onto his mount.

At least half of the camp were similarly ready, including Major Cunningham.

"Downriver!" he called. "Let's go!"

This would be the perfect opportunity to slip away, in the commotion. Jed edged Daisy away from the river, but the cypress swamp hedged them all in. There'd be no hurrying off in this part of the woods.

"Did you have aught to do with this?" came a snarl, nearly at his elbow, and Jed snapped around to find Cunningham at his flank.

And a familiar bloodlust in his eyes.

"I did not!" he threw back, nudging Daisy on, already plunging as fast as she could through the knee-deep black water.

Cunningham's great red horse matched them, lunge for lunge, and pulled ahead. The big man's attention did not waver. "I've watched you. Avowed your desire for retribution, but have you yet killed even one man?"

Jed gritted his teeth and dodged a low-hanging cypress limb. "I swear to you, I am true!"

They gained more solid ground, the horses heaving themselves up the bank, shoulder to shoulder. Cunningham rounded on him, the big horse nearly knocking Daisy back into the swamp. "True to whom, I wonder? And what?"

Jed met his gaze full on, held it despite the curling, reckless grin creasing Cunningham's face, then reined Daisy in amongst the stream of mounted men as they pushed past. "We haven't time for this."

Cunningham's mocking laugh followed him, almost lost in the sound of their flight. 'Twould be too easy to pull out a pistol and simply shoot the man. But the others would be on him in a moment—and he had too much reason now to live.

Oh Lizzy...

They broke in on the edges of the next camp downriver, already at a state of alarm and mounting up, and kept going. The cool morning worked to their advantage but 'twas only a matter of time before they needed to halt and rest the horses.

Mercy, oh God. Mercy.

On they forged, through another swamp, another creek. At the next camp after that, they did stop, the horses blowing, their breath clouds of steam in the cold air.

While the camp finished breaking and the men trailing behind caught up, Cunningham swung once more to face Jed. "I still say, something about you don't feel right."

Jed held himself still and as calm as he could be. "You challenge me, then, because of my attention to Lizzy?"

Cunningham's hand strayed toward the sword at his side, and a raw chuckle rumbled from him.

A few of the other men gathered to watch.

"Not simply that, although it's curious enough." Laughter, albeit tense, rippled around them.

Jed snorted. "If you cared a whit for her—"

Cunningham nudged his horse closer. "So, this is about love now? When you came to us—why?" He turned to Kittery, hovering near with the others ringing them. "You there—you've ridden close by him these last weeks. What say you about where his loyalties lie?"

Jed's heart pounded. *Please, Lord... Please, Lord... Please, Lord...*

"He's been all right," Kittery said slowly, the shifting of his horse betraying his own sudden nervousness. "Lacking a bit when it comes to keeping his prisoners, but—"

Cunningham's face hardened. "Keeping prisoners?"

"We was all giving him a rough time of it that one night—didn't you hear? He lost two in a day."

Jed felt his face blanch even further than it had, if that were possible. "I shot one, not that you seen it."

Kittery gave a short laugh. "So you claimed."

In truth, Jed had lagged behind the main group with the man he'd dragged away at gunpoint. Once the others were out of sight, he'd told the man to run for his life and then shot deliberately away from him.

A simple way to save a man's life. None could prove he hadn't shot him…but neither could he prove he had, either.

Was it his imagination, or had the circle of riders tightened about him?

"But you *lost* the other." Cunningham leaned toward him. "My company does not simply lose prisoners. Perhaps you mistake us, but neither do we take prisoners, for that matter."

Another round of hard-edged chuckles.

"I'll not let it happen again," Jed said tightly.

That feral grin lit Cunningham's face once more. "Aye, you'll not."

Jed reached for his pistol at the same time Cunningham drew his sabre, but his shot went wild. He parried the blade's edge with the underside of the pistol, and seizing Cunningham's coat, yanked the man from his horse.

They fell in an untidy heap. Cunningham scrabbled for the sword. Jed kicked it away. Around them, the horses shied, the men yelling and whooping. Cunningham snarled and landed a hard punch to Jed's jaw.

For Lizzy, then. For the sake of all that's true and holy.

Jed fought with a strength born of desperation, landing as many blows as he took. He tried to give himself space to draw the other pistol, but Cunningham was relentless.

Lungs burning, he swung and missed. Desperation was not enough when his opponent was taller, heavier, more driven by his need to shed blood.

Not to mention the need to punish those from whom he perceived offense.

Cunningham's elbow cracked Jed's skull. Jed staggered, and a crushing weight took hold of his throat. The morning light seemed to dim, the shouts of the men fading.

God in heaven…mercy.

A cry cut across all others. "Pickens! Pickens is coming. You must fly, again!"

With a last burst of determination, Jed scrabbled

and came up with the knife at Cunningham's belt. Swung. Stabbed.

A roar, and release from the pressure across his throat.

"No time for this!" a hoarse voice insisted.

He fell, spent.

God...mercy.

~*~*~*~

A grey morning indeed it had been, just three days after the tavern burning, and a grey noon it remained. Lizzy could not find it within herself to be sorrowful, however, despite scrubbing the floor on her knees, in someone else's establishment, in someone else's clothing, at that.

Clothing which fit, though worn. And a proper cap, with her hair pinned up beneath.

For the first time in a very long time, her feelings were, in fact, very near what she might even term *hope.* Despite the gnawing fear for Jed.

As she dipped her brush in the pail and returned to the wet edge of the planking, a man's shadow darkened the front door. Mr. Elliot leaned inside and beckoned to her. "Come, Miss Cunningham. And quickly."

She climbed to her feet and wiped her hands on her apron, then scurried after him.

A horse-drawn wagon stood in the yard, a pair of saddle horses tethered to the side. The driver nodded and touched the brim of his plain felt hat as Lizzy approached in Mr. Elliot's wake.

And then she glimpsed the booted feet sticking

out the far end of the wagon.

"I'm sorry to deliver him in this condition," Mr. Elliot said gravely. "But I think—"

With a cry, she flew the last few steps to peer over the edge of the wagon. Blood, mud, and dried leaves matted the fair hair and short beard, and what skin she could see was mottled by cuts and bruises. His filthy, torn hunting shirt lay open, the rest of his clothing in not much better condition. But the waistcoat she thought she recognized—

Swollen eyelids cracked open to reveal blue eyes. "Lizzy?"

"Jed!" She scrambled up the wheel and into the wagon, then knelt beside him in the narrow space, trembling so much she could hardly grasp his hand. "What have they done to you?"

His breathing suddenly labored, he winced. "Nothing—too bad."

Her hand skimmed his face, brushing away the debris, assessing the damage. "Oh Jed—"

"Don't cry, Lizzy. I didn't mean to make you cry. I only—wanted to make it back—to see you smile—"

He grimaced again, shifting and then arching against the hard wood of the wagon bed.

"I'm not crying," she said—but she was. Deep, gulping sobs—again. She bent until her forehead rested against his chest, but gently. "Oh Jed, I was so sure he'd kill you."

He hiccupped—was that a chuckle? "He—tried."

She cried harder.

His free hand came up to rest against her shoulder. "Shh. Sweet Elizabeth…"

"You're a simpleton and a dolt," she sobbed, lifting her head again.

He only smiled, and his eyes drifted closed.

Mopping her face with her apron, she looked over at Mr. Elliot, who appeared to be fighting a grin. "How bad is it? Truly?"

He sobered. "Bad enough. But he should make a full recovery." His dark gaze held hers for a long moment. "Because of your bravery, we were able to mount a party of men strong enough to hunt your cousin and his band where they were hiding along the Edistoes. And thus we found Jed, left behind as you see him when the rest fled downriver. He hasn't been able to tell me yet how he escaped being cut to pieces—" Mr. Elliot shook his head, and a faint smile returned. "But do I rightly assume that you're willing to help nurse him back to health?"

Chapter 14

Waking hurt. So did the sunlight, slanting from the nearby window, searing his eyes.

But the hurt meant he was alive. And alive meant hope that—

He looked around. A real bed, in a tidy room complete with washstand, chest, and beside him a chair, where a girl sat, head bent over a piece of sewing.

A girl he nearly didn't recognize, for the serenity of her face, and the proper cap covering her hair.

"Lizzy?"

She looked up, gave a little gasp, and set aside the stitchery. "Jed! How are you feeling?"

"I—" His voice failed, and she reached for a cup on the bedside table, helped him to drink. That accomplished, he sank back. As good as the cool water tasted, better still was the sight of her.

"Terrible," he admitted.

Leaning near, she examined his face, then met his eyes. A shy smile curved her mouth, chasing some of the shadows from her gaze.

"Ahh, aye. That. That was what I longed to see."

She laughed—outright, ducking her head then lifting it again. "Idiot." White teeth caught her bottom lip and tugged on it.

He laughed, too, but silently because it hurt. He reached a hand toward her, palm upward, and after the slightest hesitation, she slid hers across it. Her eyes rounded in wonder.

"How did you survive?" she breathed.

He gave a slow wag of the head. "God's own mercy."

Her lips parted and trembled, but just as she would have spoken, a knock came to the door and it opened to Zach Elliot. A broad grin creased his face. "At last! So good to see you awake."

Jed made to release Lizzy's hand and reach for Elliot's, but the other man laughed and shook his head. "Nay, stay put. You took quite a beating."

"I see that," Jed said drily, and regained Lizzy's grasp.

Some of the gravity returned to Elliot's face. "You seemed to be having trouble extricating yourself, there near the end."

Jed huffed. "I couldn't get away for anything. Cunningham decided, partly because of Lizzy, that I best be kept under close watch. And then he became suspicious—whether on her behalf or nay, I don't know—but 'twas near the end of me, I'm sure."

Elliot nodded. "You must know, your girl here walked all the way to Dawson's Station and gave me the intelligence which made it possible for Pickens to find Cunningham's camps."

"Our tavern was burned," she muttered. "Where else could I go?"

"Your—" Jed looked from one to the other, then winced. "Lizzy, what happened?"

"Our neighbors had enough of our Tory ways," she said tartly, then went on more quietly, "They had the good grace at least to let us take what we could carry."

"And your father and brothers?"

"In gaol." Elliot's mouth flattened. "They'll be sent on to Charles Town shortly."

Jed considered Lizzy's grave expression, the dip of her lashes. "And you, sweet Elizabeth? What do you wish to do?"

Her eyes came to his, watery pools reflecting, as he had observed before, all the colors of a Carolina autumn day. A dozen emotions crossed her face as her lips parted, firmed, and then parted again.

If he could just kiss her, he was sure all the aches would simply melt away. At least for a moment.

But he had to wait for her to reply.

Or did he?

And Elliot just stood there with a mocking smile. "I told her, your cousin and his wife would likely take her in until she finds a good situation for herself. It's far enough she'd not have fear of anyone finding her. Did you have aught else in mind?"

Jed swallowed. Met Lizzy's eyes again. "I told you that last morning to consider my words a proposal—but you don't have to marry me. Not if you've no wish to. My cousin and his wife would indeed be glad to have you, and—"

She laid her fingers across his lips, cool and soothing. "'Tis—'tis all right if you've changed your mind."

What? No—he shook his head but the pain lanced through him again, forcing his eyes shut. "Nay, Lizzy, I—haven't."

Her fingers flexed against his palm, and he

squeezed back, holding the clasp loosely, in case she was prepared to release him.

"Well," Elliot said briskly, "now that we have all that settled." Grin still firmly in place, he pulled a packet from his waistcoat and held it out to Jed. "Given your injuries, I've taken the liberty of arranging your furlough from the Continental Army, along with a pass, should you need it, for travel to Virginia whenever you are ready. And there is mention of your wife accompanying you. Whether or not you choose to make that so, in fact, is your business."

Jed accepted the packet with a nod. "I am sorry I did not finish the task I set out to accomplish."

"Oh, on the contrary. Because of your connection with this brave lady, we were able to put Cunningham and his boys to flight, all the way to Charles Town. I'm told he may have sustained injuries of his own. He'll not soon venture back out. And in the meantime, we're determined to guard the enemy lines more closely."

He could hardly think for the wash of relief. "You're saying I succeeded?"

"Aye, and well. Even if you did get yourself nearly killed."

"He blamed me for the attack." Jed breathed another weak laugh. "An accusation I am happy now to accept."

Lizzy sat nearly folded in on herself, one hand over her mouth.

"I am," he insisted. "If it means you're finally freed from that particular tyranny—"

Elliot nodded. "Exactly so. And I will take my

leave, until later. I'm sure the two of you have plenty to say to each other."

He bowed and left the room.

Lizzy did not move. Jed let his gaze skim the pert oval of her face, the smooth line of her neck and upper shoulder, the blue gown that fit her more neatly than the old brown one. "You're looking very well."

She glanced away, straightened on her chair. Tried to take back her hand, but he tightened his grip. "Mistress Dawson very kindly lent me some clothing." She took an unsteady breath and narrowed her gaze upon him. "So, your intent all along was to use me to get to Billy?"

"What—nay!" Oh, this girl's mind was faster than he could keep pace, at this point. "Never. I promise." He pressed her hand for emphasis. "I meant every word, Lizzy. Every word. Including the proposal."

She sat, hardly moving, but her eyes welled with tears.

"Sweet Elizabeth. You are lovely. You are brave. And I'd be most honored if you'd be my wife. That is—if you can bear being wed to a rebel."

"Your family," she said faintly. "They are rebel as well?"

"They are. But they are good people."

She sniffled. "Mr. Elliot assured me that was so." Her shoulders rose and fell with another deep breath. "And just what was your occupation before the war?"

A grin tugged at his mouth. "I was a wagonmaster. Hauled goods all up and down the

Great Road from Philadelphia to Charlotte Town. May be a while yet before I can return to that, but—"

Lizzy nodded, then swiped at her eyes and looked out the window. The tears overflowed, though she dashed them away. "He answered my prayer."

His thoughts stuttered. "Your prayer?"

Her head bobbed. Her watery gaze bounced to his and away. "You—told me to trust the Almighty. I—asked Him—to bring you back to me." She swallowed. "And He did."

Something in his own heart warmed and unfurled. He wove his fingers more firmly with hers. "I asked Him the same thing. To bring me safely back to you. So, aye, I would agree—He answered both our prayers."

Her chin tucked, she peered at him again. "I can't remember Him ever doing anything for me, before."

"Sweet Elizabeth," he breathed. "I'm sure He must have."

She swayed in her chair. "You'll not break if—I touch you?"

At last! "Not at all," he murmured gruffly, and tugged her into his arms for that long-awaited kiss.

As he thought, the pain receded.

At least for the moment.

She drew away a little and smiled. "I would be honored to accept your proposal, Jedidiah Williams."

He grinned and brushed a strand of hair from her face. "'Tis Jedidiah Wheeler. If you don't mind, that is. Making you Mistress Wheeler."

She murmured the name. "I like the sound of that."

With another smile, she kissed him again.

Epilogue

1782, the Shenandoah Valley

Brewster's Inn fairly hummed, as it always did on a busy summer's morning when filled to bursting with travelers on their way up and down the Great Road between Philadelphia and Charlotte Town.

Across the table, Sally kneaded and shaped small loaves of bread, while Lizzy rolled pie crust that would become an after-luncheon offering. Behind her, two small boys, one still in skirts and the other newly breeched, sat in the corner and took turns beating on overturned pans with a pair of wooden spoons. Sally spared them hardly a glance, but Lizzy laughed and shook her head in wonder at the commotion.

She was still not quite used to it—but 'twas a joy to belong. To be part of a family that seemed to truly value the contribution others made.

Jacky, the youngest of Sally's twin brothers, ducked under the doorjamb, holding an empty platter. "More sweet breads to the common room!"

"I'll get it," Lizzy said, and headed to replenish the platter from where more of the glazed rolls sat cooling on a side table.

The kitchen became abruptly crowded when Jed shouldered his way past Jacky, followed by his stockier but slightly shorter cousin, Sam. Blue eyes sparkling, Sam angled toward Sally, while Jed made a beeline for Lizzy.

"Hie! I'm trying to work," she protested, but leaned into his warm strength, savoring the contrast of rough and soft in his kiss, and breathing deeply of his scent of sunshine and fresh hay.

Laughing, he pulled back just enough to peer into her eyes. "And doing a fine job of it. How fares my darling wife this morning?"

Behind him, Lizzy caught a glimpse of Sam similarly embracing Sally, his big hands tenderly cradling her very round belly. She smiled and refocused on Jed's roguish grin. "I am very well, thank you."

A softer kiss this time. "And the newest little Wheeler is similarly well?"

She smiled despite the warming of her cheeks. And what a joy to have a man who seemed to hold her as his greatest treasure. "He is, indeed."

Jed chuckled. "Or she. A daughter would not be amiss, you know."

"We'll see," she said pertly, and lifted the platter.

In the buzzing common room, Lizzy made her way to the sideboard and set down her burden, then glanced to see what else needed refilling. A full array of travelers they had, and hearty appetites all. She and Sally would be cooking for hours yet.

As she turned to go back to the kitchen, a man spoke from the table next to her. "Hey! 'Tis—I can hardly believe it—but is that Lizzy Cunningham?"

Lifting her chin, she regarded him with all the reserve she could muster.

"What are you doing so far from home, Lizzy?"

the other said.

An ordinary pair of men, they were, who could be familiar, but she could not immediately recall their names. She flashed them both an arch smile. "My apologies, good sirs. You must be mistaken. I am Elizabeth Wheeler, not Lizzy Cunningham. And this is my home."

With that, she hastened back to the kitchen.

Author's Note

In real history, not all loose ends are neatly tied up, nor do all villains meet a satisfyingly just end. Major William Cunningham, dubbed "Bloody Bill" in later accounts, was an actual historical figure whose atrocities are well documented. I might have taken dramatic license on the timing, but I've rendered the actual events as faithfully as I could. Bloody Bill and his men were indeed never again the terror they had been to the South Carolina backcountry after their retreat on December 20, 1781. When his lands in Saluda County were confiscated by the U.S. government late in 1782, and the British made their final withdrawal from Charleston in December of the same year, Cunningham fled to East Florida, where he lived as an outlaw until he and his men were arrested and tried in Havana for crimes against the Spanish government. Exiled from Florida, he then turned to his cousin Robert Cunningham (not the one mentioned in this story) in the Bahamas, where he died of some tropical malady on January 18, 1787.

There's no mention of him sustaining any injury during the attack by Colonel Pickens and his militia, but where history is silent, we storytellers have room for embellishment. As it is, the facts make it abundantly clear that anyone who tried to infiltrate his regiment would have been fortunate indeed to escape alive. There was record, however, of one follower letting a prisoner go, nearly as I've described, so maybe there was a Jed somewhere among the ranks. We may never know.

~*~*~

If you've read all three stories in *Frontiers of Liberty,* thank you for journeying with me up and down the Great Wagon Road of Virginia, then to the Overmountain settlements of what is now east Tennessee, and finally through the backcountry of South Carolina. It was fun to change up the order these stories so we end up approximately where we started—at Brewster's in the Shenandoah Valley. And did you catch that Jed's contact is none other than Micah Elliot's brother-turned-rebel? Maybe someday I'll get to write his story as well.

About the Author

Transplanted to the far north after more than two decades in the Deep South, Shannon McNear loves losing herself in local history. She's the author of four novellas and six full-length novels, with the honor of a 2014 RITA® nominee and a 2021 SELAH winner among them. Yet her greatest joy is in being a military wife, mom of eight, mother-in-law of five (soon to be six), and grammie of six (soon to be eight). She's also a contributor to Colonial Quills and a member of American Christian Fiction Writers and Faith-Hope-Love Christian Writers. When not cooking, researching, or leaking story from her fingertips, she enjoys being outdoors, basking in the beauty of the northern prairies.

Also by Shannon:

The Cumberland Bride (Daughters of the Mayflower #5)

The Rebel Bride (Daughters of the Mayflower #10)

The Blue Cloak (True Colors Crime #5)

The Wise Guy and the Star (novella) in *Love's Pure Light Collection* (with Susanne Dietze, Janine Rosche, and Deborah Raney)

Daughters of the Lost Colony:
Elinor
Mary
Rebecca

More information about Shannon and her stories, including research links and events of interest, can be found at her website: shannonmcnear.com

Made in United States
North Haven, CT
28 April 2024

51883524R00157